Miracle in Black

ANITA K. GREENE

Miracle in Black
An Original work by Anita K. Greene

Published by Cedar Lake Studio
Copyright © 2017 by Anita K. Greene

ISBN 978-0-9886709-7-6

Cover Design by Wicked Smart Designs
Interior Formatting by Author E.M.S.

Published in the United States of America.

In memory of my father, Joseph Gavitt.

Always in my heart.

He who fears the Lord has a secure fortress,
and for his children it will be a refuge.

Proverbs 14:26

Miracle in Black

Chapter One

Terror clawed at the back of Carrie's throat. She glanced in her rearview mirror at the black SUV following her. Stomping on the gas pedal, she prayed for more speed. The pedal was flush to the vibrating floor but nothing was happening. Her ancient station wagon refused to go faster. *God, help me.*

Heart-pounding fear blocked her ears to all but the thought screaming through her mind. *Please, God, keep Benny safe.* Her vision blurred. She swiped at her tears and peeked over her shoulder to check on her baby snuggled in his car seat.

Up ahead the traffic light changed to yellow. She clutched the steering wheel and leaned forward, willing the cars in front of her to keep moving. The light blinked to red as she slipped beneath it.

Fighting to stay calm, she turned onto Margin Street. The old homes lining the street like elderly matrons, faded and past their prime, were blurs as tears filled her eyes and raw sobs tore at her throat. She wheeled into her driveway, tires spewing gravel. Jamming on the brakes, she felt the car groan to a halt.

The car door squealed as she lunged out, yanked on the back door, and fumbled with Benny's safety harness. He yowled, beating the air with his fists, protesting the rough handling.

"Shhh, baby. Shhh." Cupping his fuzzy head in her hand, she nestled his padded bottom in the crook of her arm and raced for the house. Reaching the top step, she stumbled on the hem of her skirt and fell to her knees. Her own cry mingled with Benny's squall. Struggling to her feet, she staggered across the wide front porch. The foyer door swung open before her. Lurching across the threshold, she crashed against a hard masculine chest clothed in a black t-shirt.

"Whoa." Big hands steadied her.

The hot rush of panic filled Carrie's chest, and she wrenched away.

The man stepped back, hands held up as though in surrender.

Crossing the foyer, Carrie juggled Benny and her keys as she unlocked her apartment door. Sparing the man closing the front door a quick glance, she slammed her apartment door and threw the deadbolt.

Shaking, she leaned against the door and buried her face in Benny's warm neck. He was safe. She'd keep him safe. That was what mothers did. They cared for their babies. Her own mother hadn't done that for her. Carrie heaved a shuddering sigh. She *was not* her mother.

"Lord, I'm afraid." Her whispered prayer sent a fresh wave of hot tears sluicing down her cheeks. Her relationship with God was still new. So was praying. Most times she felt as though she was talking to herself, but Pastor Peter encouraged her to keep at it, so she did—especially when life was crazy scary—like it was this minute.

In the depths of Benny's diaper bag, her phone chimed.

Digging beneath disposable diapers, she found the simple flip phone. The number on the screen sent chills down her spine. She wouldn't answer the call. Not now. Not ever.

Aaron Black stood to one side of the narrow window framing the front door. His eyes hunted the length of the street. He zeroed in on a black SUV with tinted windows sitting at the curb.

Gut wrenching sobs penetrated the walls of the ground floor apartment, causing his chest to squeeze in the vicinity of where he'd once had a heart. The woman reeked of terror. She'd been running long before she hit the porch. Coming down the stairs from his apartment, he'd heard the squeal of tires. When he opened the front door his first impression had been an abundance of red-gold hair and the greenest eyes he'd ever seen. She held a roaring bundle of baby.

His gut twisted. This setup was no good. He should have asked about kids before renting the place. Especially babies. His priority was to get his head together. The last thing he needed was someone else's drama.

The SUV idled curbside for twenty minutes before pulling away.

Calling himself every kind of fool, he rapped on the woman's apartment door. He heard a whisper of movement and felt her presence, but she didn't respond.

He scrubbed a hand across his face. *Walk away, Black. Just leave.* Tapping again, he leaned closer, certain she stood on the other side. "SUV's gone."

The rustle of clothing followed her breathy gasp.

"You okay in there?"

"Go away."

Well, that's gratitude for you. Swallowing a caustic remark, he whirled away then stopped. She'd be constantly running from him if he didn't introduce himself. For whatever stupid reason, that scenario didn't sit well with him. "Can't. I live upstairs."

"Upstairs is empty." Her voice wobbled.

"Not any more. I moved in this morning."

The knob rattled, and the door opened a crack. Above the security chain, one vivid green eye peered at him. "Mr. Reynolds would've told me."

"Was kinda sudden. The place is exactly what I wanted." *Cheap and fully furnished.* Because he carried only a duffle filled with a few changes of clothes, the commotion that accompanied new neighbors moving in wasn't happening.

"By the way, I'm Aaron Black." He held out his hand, hoping she'd get the hint and open the door.

She didn't.

"I'm Carrie Lillibridge. Pleased to meet you."

Not. "Yeah, same here." He paused. "If someone's bothering you, why don't you call the police?" The minute he said the words, he wished he could stuff them back into his mouth.

Her eyebrow shot up and panic flared in the depth of that green eye seconds before she slammed the door in his face.

Running a hand around the back of his neck, he walked out the front door. "Welcome to the neighborhood, Black."

Chapter Two

Machinery clanked and a motor squealed, setting his teeth on edge. Every second counted. He saw her—red-gold hair flying. The baby. She didn't have to remind him. His assignment was to extract the child and keep him safe when the bust went down. Sweat ran into his eyes. An explosion reverberated through the building. Flames roared into the air.

Aaron lurched out of bed, drenched in sweat. He pulled air into his lungs, working to lower his heart rate. *The dream. Again.* Only this time, *she* appeared in it.

The whine of an engine refusing to turn over drifted through his open bedroom window. He pushed aside the curtain. In the driveway below, the beat-up gray station wagon's engine wouldn't fire. The woman was gonna burn out the starter, for crying out loud. Grabbing yesterday's jeans, he hiked them up over his muscular legs and headed for the door, zipping and buttoning as he went.

Barefoot, he hopped and high-stepped across the rough gravel driveway trying to avoid the largest rocks. He pounded a fist on the roof of the car to gain her attention. "You're gonna burn out the starter!"

She frowned at him and twisted the key again.

Women! He rubbed a hand across his chest in frustration.

Her eyes tracked the movement, and her cheeks pinked before she jerked her gaze to his face.

In a calmer tone, he tried again. "Pop the hood. Let me take a look." Not waiting for an answer he walked to the front of the car, rapped his knuckles on the hood, and gestured for her to open it.

She glared at him through the windshield.

Fine. If she wanted a stare-down he'd be happy to oblige. He crossed his arms and returned her glare. Standing on a particularly sharp rock, he was thankful when she released the catch with an angry yank. He raised the hood and leaned over the engine.

The car door squealed, and her footsteps crunched over the stones. "What are you doing?"

Aaron glanced up. The sunlit fire in her hair almost blinded him. Suspicion radiated from her reminding him of an orange kitten he'd pulled from a dumpster. All hiss and spit.

"Trying to find the trouble." He checked the distributor cap. Belatedly, he added, "In the engine." He'd already found a peck of trouble that had nothing to do with the car and everything to do with the woman standing beside him.

"I have to go to work." Her belted lavender dress emphasized lush curves.

He never considered himself a fashion police, but her dress resembled one from his grandmother's closet. "You're not going anywhere until I figure out the problem."

She let out a huff of annoyance and glanced at her watch.

"Don't push my buttons, lady." He slammed the hood with force. "You woke me making a racket. I haven't had my coffee, and," he walked to the driver's car door, "the rocks are killing my feet."

"Punctuality is important to me, Mr. Black."

He dropped into the driver's seat and rotated the key part way, scanning the gauges. "Is that so, Ms. Lillibridge?" He dropped his hand to his thigh and sat quiet for a moment before saying, "I found your problem."

"You did?" Eyes wide, her soft tone matched his. "What is it?"

Jaw clenched, Aaron launched his big body out of the car. "You're outta gas."

"Oh." Her cheeks blushed a rosy pink.

"You were running on fumes when you pulled in here last night." The volume of his voice was set on "bellow." He didn't like to bellow. Not at pretty women, anyway.

Her embarrassment changed to dazed awe. "Fumes?"

"The fuel needle is below E."

She burst into laughter. Side splitting, wipe-away-tears laughter. "That's amazing." She shifted her bright gaze to him. "He did answer!"

Well, that explained precisely nothing. Arms crossed, feet braced apart, he pinned her with his best hard cop stare. He'd regret this. "Who answered and what was the question?"

She laughed so hard she leaned against the car. The woman was certifiable.

"God. He answered my prayers."

Aaron snorted. "Yeah. A regular miracle on Margin Street." He didn't believe in miracles. He wasn't sure he believed in God anymore.

"Yes." Switching from ecstatic to defensive in two point three seconds, she faced him. "I couldn't make the car go faster...."

"No gas."

"...To get away from him."

"Who?" She knew. He was sure of that. *Stay out of it,*

Black. He ignored his own advice. "Why did he follow you home?"

She seemed to shrink before his eyes. Her spark drained away, and he felt like he'd kicked a puppy. The woman was driving him crazy. Bad guys were right up his alley. He dealt with them every day on the job. When he had a job.

"It's none of your business."

"I live here now. I'm making it my business. If I see that vehicle again, I'll call the police."

"No!" She grabbed his arm. "Please don't do that."

There it was again. The same terror he'd witnessed last night when she ran into him at the door. The hand gripping his arm was small and pale against his bronzed skin. He ran a finger across her knuckles. She shivered and surprise flared in her eyes. Before she could withdraw, he rested his hand on hers. "Give me one good reason not to call them."

"I don't want police involved."

"Why not?"

She pulled her hand away. "I don't trust them. Okay?"

No, that wasn't okay, but for now he'd keep his mouth shut about his chosen profession. "What have you got against the police?" He paused. "Or maybe the question should be, what have they got against you?"

Carrie pivoted away only to be spun back around. His musky scent enveloped her. Above his heart, a puckered white scar marked an old injury. "I have to get to work." She couldn't hold his gaze so trained her eyes on his chest. *Big mistake.*

He heaved an irritated huff. Muscle overlaid with sun-kissed skin rose and fell.

"Give me a minute to slip on my shirt and shoes. I'll go to the corner station and fill a gas can for you."

"You don't have to do that. I can go."

"Stay put."

"You're very good at issuing orders."

He frowned and scanned the street. "You want to be vulnerable out there?" He glanced into the car at the empty infant seat. "Where's your baby?"

She waved a hand toward the pink cottage next door. With a purple door and white gingerbread lacing the eaves it always made her think of fairytales. "Next door at Aunt Thelma's."

Giving a curt nod, he headed back across the drive to the house, the stones obviously hurting his soles as he tried to step lightly.

Serves him right, sticking his nose where it doesn't belong. Trying to outrun her unkind thought, Carrie hurried to her neighbor's house.

The purple door opened, and Aunt Thelma stepped out onto the porch with Benny in her arms. "Carrie, what's wrong? I saw you talking to that young man."

With love and compassion, Thelma Bray had become an honorary aunt to Carrie and her baby. At seventy-two years old, the retired hairdresser was a spry, cheerful woman and the only person to ever invite Carrie to church.

"He's my upstairs neighbor, Auntie. Guess what? A miracle happened to me!" Carrie still couldn't believe it. Grumpy Aaron Black could keep his opinions to himself. "I ran out of gas yesterday and still made it home."

"Well...yes, I suppose that could be a miracle." Aunt Thelma smiled. Her lipstick had bled into the tiny wrinkles rimming her lips.

Carrie took Benny. "Hi, sweetie. Mr. Black offered to get

a can of gas for my car." She followed Thelma inside and stood beside her at the window.

Aaron came out of the house to begin his trek to the corner gas station.

Beneath her thick eyeliner and blue eye shadow, Thelma's eyes sparkled. "He's handsome. Wish I were younger."

Snuggling Benny, Carrie glanced at her friend and mentor. "The man is off limits for me."

Thelma patted her arm. "Don't let one bad relationship distort your view of all men, dear. God may have plans for you and your baby that includes a wonderful man."

Carrie kissed the old woman's papery cheek painted with a dollop of rouge. "Perhaps." *But not likely. Not if I have any say in the matter.* Changing the topic, she asked about Thelma's many grandchildren. For the next ten minutes, she admired pictures and heard about their latest escapades.

Before Thelma could pull out the fifth packet of pictures, heavy footsteps clumped across her porch.

"He's back." Thelma opened the door. "Hello, young man. I'm Thelma Bray. We were talking about you."

Carrie groaned.

"Then you know I'm Aaron Black, your new neighbor." His dark gaze swept the room before resting on Carrie. "You're all set."

Giving Benny a kiss, she handed him to Thelma. "Thank you, Mr. Black." His steady gaze caused her heart to flip-flop.

He followed her down the steps, keeping pace at her side. She wished he'd go away. She didn't like butterflies, but a kaleidoscope of them were flitting about in her belly.

"Do you take the same route to and from work every day?" His hand rested on the car door handle.

"Yes."

"You should try varying your route." He opened the door and waited for her to settle in before closing it.

The car started, and Carrie heaved a sigh of relief. Without money for repairs she didn't know what she'd do if it broke down. She put the car in gear and pulled away, glancing once in her rearview mirror.

Aaron Black stood in the driveway watching her leave.

A warm sensation settled in her tummy. *Is this what it feels like to be cared for?* "You can wipe that stupid idea from your mind, Carrie Anne Lillibridge."

Chapter Three

Beneath the relentless heat of the afternoon sun, Aaron's damp t-shirt clung to his shoulders. Sweat soaked the red bandana tied across his brow. Squatting beside his bike, he rubbed a soft cloth along the chrome exhaust pipe. Too bad his life couldn't be cleaned up as easily as his bike.

Not fit for duty.

His stomach knotted every time he thought about the chief standing behind his desk—Aaron's psych eval in hand.

"Take three months off, Black. Relax and try to get yourself together." He'd been adamant. Men and operations would be at risk if Aaron continued to work.

Aaron wiped at a dot of grease on the chrome. His assignment had been to keep a child out of harm's way. But things had gone from bad to worse. Swallowing the sour taste of failure, he rubbed harder at the already spotless chrome. He'd hoped a change of scenery would help, so he'd hit the road. Heading east, he rode until he couldn't go any farther without flooding the engine of his bike in the Atlantic Ocean. He ended up in a small town on the Rhode Island seacoast, living above a woman with a life as unsettled as his own. *And she has a baby.*

Aaron's heart lurched painfully. He'd always thought he'd have a family some day. But now, just thinking about it sent shooting pains through his chest. Taking on the huge responsibility of a baby no longer held appeal. No way. No how. Alone. That's how he was gonna live and die.

He tossed the rag aside. But here he was. Kneeling in the driveway pretending to work on his bike while listening for the whine of the old station wagon's engine. The thing needed a new transmission. Not that it was any of his business. Ms. Carrie Lillibridge would be the first to tell him that very thing. She didn't need a head case like him in her life. But the cop in him wanted to be close in case she was followed home again. He wanted the license plate number. His interest had nothing to do with her bright smile or her tenderness when she held her baby.

The squeal of tires sent him sprinting to the curb.

Carrie's car roared up the street, the SUV close behind.

She cut into the driveway, forcing Aaron to jump back. Bits of grass flew up, and the trashcans rocked in her wake.

The SUV slowed before shooting past.

Mud. The license plates were caked with the stuff though the state was suffering through a drought.

The vehicle cut around the next corner and raced out of sight.

Aaron whipped around and ran to Carrie. "You okay?"

She dove out of the car and hurried toward Thelma's house. The freckles dusting her checks were bright against the pallor of her skin. "Do I look like I'm okay?" She wore three-inch heels with pointy toes, and with each step she wobbled like a top at the end of its spin cycle.

He placed a steadying hand under her elbow. "You can

slow down. He left." Afraid she'd fall, he stuck with her across the uneven lawn and up Thelma's porch steps.

She knocked once before walking in. "Auntie?"

"Back here."

Aaron followed her into the baby's room. The heavy sweet scent of clean baby engulfed him as the women cooed and fussed over the little rascal lying on the bed dressed in nothing but a diaper. An odd curling sensation warmed his gut. "Hustle it up and dress him."

The women stared at him as though he'd sprouted an extra head.

"I want to know you're safe at home."

"Carrie?" Thelma's gaze shifted between them. "What's wrong?"

Sparkly green daggers zinged his way. *Uh oh.*

"Noth—"

"Tell her, Carrie, or I will." Aaron crossed his arms.

Her jaw flapped a few times, but no words came out.

He could wait.

Carrie fought to tamp down her anger. Of all the bullheaded, overbearing men! She picked up the diaper bag and stuffed the changing pad and assorted baby gear inside.

Thelma laid a hand on her arm. "Carrie?"

Carrie glanced at Aaron. His mouth slanted in an uncompromising slash. "Someone followed me home."

Thelma gasped. "Who?"

Aaron quirked an eyebrow. "Yes, Carrie. Who?"

She snapped the blanket and folded it. "I don't know...exactly."

Thelma's outrage drowned out Aaron's snort of disbelief.

"You should call the police. Where's my phone?" A gnarled hand on the baby's belly, Thelma glanced around the room in search of her cordless phone. "I can never remember where I leave the thing."

Carrie finished packing the diaper bag. "That's okay, Auntie. I'll go home. I'm sure everything is okay." She glared at Aaron, daring him to contradict her.

Ignoring her, he addressed Thelma. "Keep your doors locked, ma'am."

"Is he watching me?"

He glanced first at the baby, then at Carrie. "I'm not sure."

Carrie fought the temptation to whack him with the loaded diaper bag. She had to get Aaron out of here before he said more to upset her friend.

Thelma fiddled with the collar of her dress and batted her crooked false eyelashes. "I'm so glad you're here, Mr. Black. You listen to him, Carrie."

Unbelievable. The woman was seventy-two! Carrie thrust the heavy bag at Aaron. She picked up Benny and kissed Thelma's cheek. "Thank you, Auntie." Elbowing her way past Aaron, she headed out the front door and marched home as best as she could in heels.

In the process of unlocking her apartment door, she heard her phone begin to chime in the diaper bag Aaron carried. He followed her inside, pawing through the bag in an attempt to locate it. "Here." He held it out to her.

Her heart dropped to her toes. *His number.* Pulling her gaze from the screen, she carried Benny to the playpen in the corner. Leaning over the railing, she placed him on a soft blanket.

"Hello?"

She almost toppled in after her baby. Aaron answered *her* phone. She clutched the side rail, her heart in her throat.

He listened intently before disconnecting the call. "Nobody there." He stepped closer. "Get calls like that often?"

Mouth dry, Carrie couldn't form the words to answer him. For every step he advanced, she retreated, fear expanding in her chest until she couldn't breathe. The green overstuffed chair bumped against the back of her shaky legs, and she sank into it.

He kept coming. Bending over her, he braced both hands on the wide padded arms of the chair. "You knew who was calling." The muscles on his jaw hardened as he clenched his teeth.

Gathering what little courage she had, she inhaled. She was done cowering. Well, as done as she could be. He'd pushed his way into her personal space scaring her spitless. "You have no right answering my phone." Her voice trembled with a bit of fear and a whole lot of fury.

"You weren't in any hurry to answer it. Tell me why."

Aaron's gut pinged. He was frightening her. A tear trickled from the corner of her eye and trailed across her temple to disappear in the red-gold hair fanned across the cushioned back of the chair.

He didn't want her to fear him. Dread for her safety ate at him as he watched the rapid beat of her pulse beneath the pale skin of her throat. The desire to shake some sense into her rolled through him, but he was afraid to touch her. Afraid he'd end up wrapping his arms around her and never letting go.

Sucking in a harsh breath, he straightened and backed away. He rubbed a hand over his buzz cut. "Help me understand." His eyes drifted around the sparsely furnished room taking in the odd assortment of furniture and doodads, searching for clues to help him unravel the mystery surrounding Carrie.

She slipped off her shoes. "Thank you for carrying Benny's bag."

The baby squirmed and fretted in the playpen.

Aaron wasn't ready to leave. Too many questions plagued him. Things he wanted to know. Like why she lived in this apartment raising her child alone? Where was Benny's father? Then there were the things he *needed* to know to keep her safe.

On the wall above the burnt orange sofa, a bullfighter painted on black velvet swirled his red cape over a charging bull. "Where'd you find the artwork?"

"A yard sale." Her hands were clasped together in her lap.

A flock of ceramic flamingos shared shelf space with a collection of white knobby bud vases. A lily lamp of art deco vintage perched on an ancient shipping trunk. The crazy patchwork of design and function had no rhyme or reason, yet all the pieces worked together. The décor reflected the complex woman living in the apartment. "Do you go to yard sales often?"

"Most Saturdays in the warm weather. Sometimes I find things for our clients."

"Clients?" Maybe he'd hit on something. "Where do you work?"

The baby's fussing cranked up a notch, bringing Carrie to her feet. Taking him from the playpen, she rocked back and forth making little clucking noises. "The Neighborhood Center."

Pushing aside a shiny gold pillow emblazoned with the

word, FLORIDA and scenic pictures, Aaron lowered himself to the couch. A broken spring poked his thigh. "Who are your clientele?"

The baby shrieked, making conversation difficult.

Carrie ignored his question and walked into the kitchen with the red-faced infant.

At the risk of losing his hearing, he followed her.

Juggling a screaming baby, she removed a bottle from the fridge and placed it in a steaming bowl of water.

Amazed by her calm in the center of Benny's stormy squall, Aaron stood back ready to pounce with more questions the moment the opportunity arose.

The bottle's nipple touched Benny's lips, and he went silent.

Carrie's warm murmuring voice curled around Aaron. *Trouble.* He was in it heart-deep. He took a step back. He'd get his answers another time.

He slipped out of her apartment, pulling the door closed and checking the lock behind him.

Carrie pulled up her shoulder length hair and wrapped a stretchy ponytail holder around the thick skein. She sighed. The holder wouldn't stay in long. Her hair lived a life of its own. Her head happened to be the one unfortunate enough to host the unruly mess.

In front of the dresser's low mirror, she rose on tiptoes for a full view of her outfit. The directors for the Center were meeting. As the receptionist, she wanted to look her best today.

She had starched the white cotton blouse into submission. An hour at the ironing board tamed the rows of tiny ruffles running down the front. The elastic band of her full skirt hugged her waist. She ran a hand over the floral fabric. When the donated skirt arrived at the Clothing Closet, Joan brought it to the office for Carrie to try on.

Finding clothes to fit her curves was a challenge. Carrie insisted on modesty. Joan called her choices "dowdy." *Whatever.*

Carrie's ex-boyfriend had demanded she wear form-fitting tops and miniscule skirts. What she thought were gifts of love and affection were nothing more than him imposing his will on her. *Control.* That's what Ross St. Martin wanted.

Now Carrie was in control. And if her hem was a little too long to be fashionable, or her clothes a bit on the baggy side, so be it. The choices were her own.

From the depths of her closet she pulled out a pair of white pumps. They were run down at the heels, but she didn't have the means to purchase a new pair. If she had grabbed her shoes when she left Ross, she wouldn't be wearing other people's castoffs.

"You did the best you could, Carrie Anne Lillibridge. And don't you forget that." She jammed her feet into the shoes and kept right on talking to herself. "You didn't have room for shoes in your pack. And besides, you wanted to take as little of what Ross gave you as possible."

Sitting on the edge of the bed, she leaned over Benny, peacefully asleep in the center of the quilt. She'd arrived at Mercy House ten months ago, carrying a backpack and a laundry basket filled with everything she owned and three months pregnant.

She kissed Benny on the forehead and placed her fingertip in the palm of his up-turned hand. Instantly his tiny fingers closed around it. "I love you," she whispered in his small pink ear. She'd loved him from the moment she discovered she was pregnant.

Ross considered the baby a complication to his plans. Ross St. Martin. Political wannabe. She'd been naïve and expected him to be excited by the news. The familiar curl of humiliation swept through her. She'd hoped he'd want to marry her.

Something thumped in the apartment overhead.

She hadn't seen Aaron again after he'd left her apartment last night. She nuzzled Benny's fat rosy cheek.

The man's bossy attitude had her snapping at him like a fishwife. Last night when he pressed her about the phone call fear had reared its ugly head. Only when he backed off, could she breathe again.

Carrie rolled to her back and stared at the ceiling, listening to the creak of floorboards and water running in the apartment overhead.

She had to get over her attraction to him. Otherwise, she'd lose herself in his dark eyes and dissolve into a complete pudding head. *No, thank you.* One crummy relationship in a lifetime was more than enough. With the help of God and friends, she had a good life. She didn't need a man, and especially not one like Aaron Black.

Annoyed with herself for mooning about, she hurried to dress Benny. Aunt Thelma couldn't babysit him today so he'd be at the Center's daycare. She loved having him there. She could run to the nursery and visit him when time and duties permitted.

Loading baby and gear into the car, she glanced over at Aaron's black and chrome Harley. For the first time she noticed it had Illinois license plates. She stepped closer and ran her fingertips across the ridges of the handgrip. She'd never ridden a motorcycle. She pivoted away, afraid to entertain the notion.

On the drive to work, she found herself comparing the motorcycles she passed to the powerful machine sitting in the driveway at home.

She was being silly. Through her open car window the hot breeze blew her hair in all directions. Clear evidence she'd once again lost a ponytail holder.

Carrie parked her car in the Center's lot and set about unbuckling Benny. One street over a big bike rumbled. She tried to find the source but the houses stood close together and had yards cluttered with toys, clotheslines, and garden sheds. She didn't see a motorcycle in any of them.

Shaking her head at her own foolishness, she took Benny from his seat. "It only sounds like his, sweetie. Your mama is a little crazy today."

Chapter Four

Aaron dumped the can of pork and beans into a dented pan and placed it on the stove. He turned the flame on high. Just what he needed to do—add more heat to the already oppressively hot apartment. Tomorrow he'd buy a fan. Tonight he'd suffer.

As he stirred the beans, his attention drifted to the bit of feminine fluff on the kitchen table. The little circle of fabric captivated him. Shiny silver threads wove through the ruffled lavender cloth.

Early this morning, Carrie had shown curiosity about his bike. Standing back from the window, he'd followed her every move wondering what was going through her unpredictable mind as she tentatively touched the handgrip. She had pulled away as though burned and spun around so fast, the stretchy cloth holding her hair slipped out and fell to the ground. Not realizing her loss, she'd left for work.

He'd raced outside determined to follow her. Before hopping on his bike, he'd retrieved the ponytail holder she lost and stuffed it in his pocket.

The scent of warm molasses drew his attention to the stove. He'd mashed the beans to a pulp with his heavy-handed stirring. Extinguishing the flame, he leaned a hip against the sink and wolfed down the goopy mess to fill the hole in his gut. Too bad nothing could repair the gaping wound left by a failed assignment. A baby had died in his arms. A baby like the one living in the apartment below him.

His stomach twisted.

He scrapped his half eaten supper into the trash and tossed the dirty dishes into the sink. The combination of heat and roiling emotion bore down on him as the walls of his apartment began to close in. Grabbing his keys, he ran down the stairs, slammed the front door, and jogged to his bike. A ride offered him a cool breeze and, for a short while, freedom from the agonizing thoughts and memories.

Footsteps thundered down the stairs. On the wall shelf, Carrie's flock of ceramic flamingos rattled. A minute later the rumble of the Harley beat against her windows.

Thankfully, she hadn't seen Aaron once today. Perhaps last night scared him away. She slapped a thick slice of ham on a bulky roll and slathered it with mustard. *Good.* She didn't want him nosing around in her business.

Her apartment was thick with hot, humid air. Benny had a full tummy and would be content for a few hours so an escape to the beach for a picnic was on the evening agenda.

Packing her sandwich in a small, insulated tote, she added a bag of chips, a peach, and a bottle of fruit juice. She slipped her Bible into Benny's diaper bag. Pulling her hair off her neck she secured it with a stretchy piece of purple cording decorated with a dangling gold heart charm.

With each step Carrie took, the sand shifted underfoot. Carrying a blanket, a diaper bag and Benny in his carrier, the load weighed her down, but she didn't mind. A few hours of cool ocean breezes and the panorama of water and sand were worth the effort.

She spread her blanket beyond the reach of the ebbing tide where waves hissed and stretched foamy fingers across the sand before racing back into the tumbling green shallows.

Most of the sun worshipers had left. On the end of the rock jetty, a fisherman cast his line into the waves. At the water's edge, a couple strolled past. The man was tall and had one arm in a sling. His other arm was wrapped around the shoulders of a petite woman carrying an adorable white puppy. They looked at each other as though the rest of the world didn't exist.

Carrie pushed aside the twinge of envy. She supposed love worked out for some people. Just not her.

Overhead, terns glided on the wind currents. On the horizon, clouds changed to pink as the sun set behind her.

She burrowed her feet into the cool damp sand found a few inches beneath the dry, sugary surface. Her Bible, propped on her legs, lay open to The Psalms. She traced her finger down the page until she found the verse she wanted.

The Lord on high is mightier than the noise of many waters, than the mighty waves of the sea.

God was bigger and more powerful than the huge expanse of water stretched before her. Setting her Bible aside, she lifted Benny from his carrier and walked to the water's edge. Schools of minnows glittered in the warm shallows. Waves lapped and tumbled over her feet before pulling away, drawing the hard-packed mud from under her heels in a ticklish flow of sand and sea.

The breeze tugged at her loose cotton blouse and khaki shorts as she waded a short distance along the beach. She collected a few pure white beach stones and nudged a stranded starfish into the water with her toe. The roll and boom of the waves lulled Benny to sleep. Retracing her steps, she placed him in his carrier and unpacked her supper.

A large pair of bare feet entered her peripheral vision. Her heart bumped against her ribs.

"Sure it's wise to be here alone?"

She knew it! They were the same feet she'd seen hopping across her driveway. Carrie leaned back and frowned up at Aaron. "Guess I'm not alone anymore." Faster than she could think to protest, he dropped to the blanket next to her.

"I'll take that as an invitation."

She should be indignant and tell him to go away, but the soothing roll of the waves had mellowed her, and she couldn't muster an argument. "Did you follow me here?"

His gaze shifted to the horizon. "When I left the house you were still there."

True. She sighed. "The evening's too beautiful to stay indoors. My apartment is airless."

His gaze drifted back to her. "Mine, too."

She searched for something to say. Holding her ham sandwich, she asked, "Want half?"

He studied the thick sandwich for a long moment.

Please take the bait. If they were stuffing bulky roll into their mouths, he couldn't interrogate her on what was becoming his favorite subject.

"Thanks. Looks good."

Yes! Using her thumbnails and fingers, she began to divide the sandwich. Half way through she gave up being neat and tore the thing apart. She handed him half of the mangled roll. *"Bon appetite."* She opened her small bag of chips and placed it on the blanket between them.

She nibbled on her half of the sandwich wanting it to last. Talking with a full mouth would be impolite.

She watched with trepidation as he stuffed the last bite into his mouth. A half of a sandwich—a *big* sandwich—had taken him only two minutes to devour. *Oh dear.*

He turned toward her.

She held out the rest of her sandwich. "Here, I'm not that hungry."

"You sure?"

She nodded.

"Thanks." His fingers grazed hers. "Tastes better than the slop I ate before I left the house."

A safe subject. *Hurray!* "What did you have?"

The muscles in his lean jaw tightened and released as he chewed the rest of her sandwich. "A can of baked beans."

What could she say about baked beans? *Which kind? With bacon? Onion? BBQ sauce?* This was not going well at all. She opened the small bottle of juice and took a swig. Wiping the lip of the bottle, she thrust it at him. "Drink?"

"Thanks."

Five gulps—she counted—and he emptied the bottle. He polished off the rest of the sandwich and wiped his mouth with the back of his hand.

She'd almost run out of food. A piece of fruit stood between her and a multitude of questions.

"Carrie—"

"Peach?" She held up her last offering.

Aaron looked at the fruit she held level with his nose. She'd shoved food at him as fast as he could eat it. "Aren't you hungry?"

She shook her head and waved the peach at him.

Had Adam felt this same unease when Eve approached with the apple? He took the peach and bit down. Juice dribbled over his lip. A paper napkin flapped about in front of his face, and he snatched it out of her hand and wiped his chin.

She peeked inside the chip bag.

She'd offer him crumbs if she had any. Finishing the peach, he chucked the pit at a seagull hanging around waiting for handouts. "Is that everything?"

"What?"

"Is that all the food?" He glanced at the baby. "You don't have anything in the diaper bag or under Benny do you?" He couldn't tell if she was puzzled or miffed. Probably both.

"Are you *still* hungry?"

"Nope. Just checking."

Panic flared in her eyes. She looked at her son asleep on her other side. The movement of her head caused the braid of elastic to slip lower on her ponytail.

"Come here often?"

She kept her face averted and shook her head.

Aaron heaved a sigh. *Now what?* "Hey." He tried to soften his voice, become less threatening. "You mad at me for eating your supper?"

She looked at him and frowned. "I offered you the food."

"So why the silent treatment?"

"I don't do silent treatments."

"So talk to me then." Aaron glanced at the baby. If the carrier hadn't hemmed her in, she'd be edging away, putting distance between them.

"About what?" She looked at him uncertainly.

"Whatever." *Just talk to me.*

She latched onto the small leather book resting on the blanket. "I was reading The Psalms before you showed up."

His heart sank and landed on all the food in his gut making him nauseous. There were only two subjects he had an aversion to. Babies and God. One slept only a few feet away, and the other was about to become the topic of conversation. *Good going, Black.*

She leafed through the Bible and ran her finger over the thin paper page. "Here. Listen to this. *For the Lord is the great God, and the great King above all gods. In His hand are the deep places of the earth; the heights of the hills are His also. The sea is His, for He made it; and His hands formed the dry land.*" She gazed at him expectantly.

He couldn't think of one honest thing to say that wouldn't set her off, but he wouldn't lie. He had a lot of marks against him. He didn't want to add another one for lying. "That's nice."

Her eyes grew round. "That's nice? That's *nice*?"

Okay, so that didn't work. His brain scrambled for another platitude.

She swept an arm toward the ocean. "Aaron, a God of power and might created all this." She shuffled her feet. Blue nail polish with silver spangles decorated her toes. "The tiny grains of sand. All this water and the creatures swimming in it."

She gave him a haven't-you-got-something-to-say look.

He figured if he said she was cute when all fired up, she probably wouldn't appreciate it. Though she was already on a roll so he might as well be honest. "I was being polite."

"You were indifferent, Aaron."

Twice. She used his name twice. "I'm glad you have faith, Carrie. The world needs people like you. But for me…I just…just…."

A tiny frown crossed her flushed face. "Don't you believe in God?"

He propped an elbow on his bent knee. "I don't have a lot to do with Him these days. I gave up on God."

"Then *you* are lucky."

He speared her with his gaze. "Why?"

She leaned toward him, her face so earnest he wanted to kiss her on the nose. "God hasn't given up on you."

The baby stirred and yawned.

Aaron glanced at him then out over the water where a fishing trawler crawled across the vast horizon. "I'm not convinced of that. Things have happened."

"What things?"

He narrowed his eyes. "Tell you what. You share your secrets and I'll share mine."

Carrie pulled back. She'd blundered into that one, big time. She huffed and took Benny out of his carrier. Resting him on her shoulder, she rubbed and patted his back. "Don't spoil a perfectly nice evening."

His eyes, dark and brooding, settled on Benny.

She surprised herself by asking, "Want to hold him?"

Aaron's whole body jerked. "No!" He crab-walked off the blanket before jumping to his feet and stepping back.

Her mouth hung open but she couldn't close it. Not while this take-charge man stood over her, his eyes wide with terror.

He spun away stripping off his t-shirt. He tossed it on the blanket. Hitting the water at a dead run, he dove into the first wave that curled toward him.

"What was that all about, Benny?" She ran a hand over the tee. The fabric held the heat of his body.

Time passed as he swam back and forth parallel to the beach using long sure strokes. At one point, a group of swimmers joined him as he pushed hard toward the stone jetty. The other swimmers used a different stroke that kept them lower in the water. Before reaching the rocks, they dove like seals and headed back to wherever they came from leaving Aaron to his solitary swim.

In the waning light, the water turned pewter. Carrie stood and folded her blanket. Time to go home and bathe the baby. She hated to leave Aaron. Swimming alone wasn't safe, but he wasn't coming in. Perhaps he was waiting for her to leave.

Disappointment spiraled through her as she began the trek to her car. At the crest of the sand dune, she looked back.

Aaron's body glistened in the last of the sunlight as he waded to shore.

Aaron watched Carrie walk over the sand dune loaded like a pack mule. Her bright hair billowed in the ocean breeze.

A pang of guilt cramped his gut. A gentleman would've helped her. Yeah, well, he never said he was a gentleman.

The look on her face when he ran away told him all he needed to know. Carrie thought he'd lost his mind.

She'd left his t-shirt. In the sand, a glint of gold caught his eye. Her ponytail holder. He pulled it up over his hand letting the heart charm dangle from his wrist.

By the time he arrived home night had fallen. The windows of Carrie's apartment glowed with a golden light.

Not ready to go inside and face the sticky heat, he strolled to the corner gas station and bought an ice cream on a stick. Anything to cool down. Calm down—though he needed more than ice cream to achieve that. How could he face her again? Running wasn't his style, but he'd put on quite the show at the beach. He hadn't expected her to offer him a chance to hold the baby.

He didn't take the direct route home, walking around the block instead. The sultry night air carried the muffled noise of televisions and the charcoal scent of grilling burgers. Up the street a dog barked and a door slammed. A peaceful evening. He'd dreamed about nights like this while working as a soldier for Uncle Sam in places no sane person would go.

Back then he talked to God, but his prayers had been angry and demanding. Chewing on the wooden ice cream stick, he shook his head. Guess not much had changed in that department. And wouldn't that shock the wide-eyed, God-fearing Ms. Lillibridge.

Aaron rounded the corner. The lights in Carrie's apartment blazed bright.

A shadow bobbed past one living room window.

He blinked to clear his vision.

A dark silhouette moved in front of the next window.

The hair on the back of Aaron's neck snapped to attention. Ducking behind a hedge for cover, he maneuvered through Thelma's yard, senses alert to every sound and movement. He'd gone through this drill many times before. This time he didn't have an eighty-pound pack on his back or a weapon in his hands.

Crouched behind Thelma's car, he watched the deep shadows close to the house. If the man was Carrie's stalker, he'd dared to leave the protective cover of his vehicle.

The creak of the back kitchen step was accompanied by the whispered rub of fabric. Aaron dropped to the ground and inched forward.

Swearing broke the night silence and rapid footsteps tripped down the steps. A thick, eye-watering stink choked Aaron as a disembodied white stripe darted from beneath the steps and undulated across the lawn straight at him.

A skunk! And he was eye level with the critter.

The prowler crashed through the hedge bordering the backyard. Aaron shot to his feet and ran after him, angry with himself for not having done any recon in the area. Sucking in a lung full of the foul musk, he struggled to breathe.

In the distance, an engine fired.

Making his way through an unfamiliar yard, Aaron arrived at the street in time to see a non-descript sedan pull away from the curb. He blinked hard but couldn't read the plate through the tears leaking from his eyes. The black SUV was nowhere in sight.

Jogging down the street, he returned to the house taking a quick survey of the area. *A little late to be checking the perimeter, wouldn't you say, Black?*

He passed Thelma's cottage where a window glowed on the second floor. Focusing his attention on Carrie's apartment, his heart stuttered. The front foyer door was open.

He dove behind the rhododendrons that lined the porch and listened. Studying the street, he berated himself for chasing the prowler when he should have checked on Carrie.

Seeing and hearing nothing, he hoisted himself over the porch rail. Avoiding the light streaming from the door, he crouched low against the exterior wall of the house and moved silently to the door. Carrie's apartment door stood open as well.

Slipping into the foyer, he killed the overhead light. Soft thumps came from Carrie's kitchen. The living room was tidy with no signs of disturbance. Did she have the baby with her?

A harsh crash and muffled scream shattered the quiet.

Aaron plunged through the door and raced to the kitchen doorway.

Chapter Five

Carrie rubbed her knee and glared at the box fan lying at her feet. She'd have a whopper of a bruise tomorrow. Wedging the cumbersome fan into the window was proving difficult. In her peripheral vision she saw movement in the doorway. She snapped around. Her heart plummeted.

Aaron crouched in the doorway in a defensive stance. His features were rigid with tension, and the air around him crackled. His hard eyes searched the room before coming back to rest on her. "You okay?"

"Yes." Goose bumps raced along her arms.

His gaze flicked to the fan then back to her. "Where's the baby?" He swept the room again with his uncompromising gaze.

"Th—the bedroom."

He pivoted and stalked out of the kitchen.

"Wait! Aaron, what's happening?"

He went into the foyer and closed and locked the front entrance door. He stepped into her living room and did the same to her apartment door. "Show me the baby." He moved toward the bedrooms.

Carrie hurried after him. "Aaron, stop!" Less than two hours ago, this man had been terrified to hold Benny. Now he was here demanding to see him? She ducked around him and stood in front of the closed bedroom door, bracing her hands on the frame. "You're frightening me."

"I'm checking on him."

"Why?"

In the narrow hall, he loomed big and dark. "Step out of my way, Carrie." He nudged her aside and opened Benny's door. "Stay here."

"Oh, I don't *think* so, buster." She didn't let his glower deter her. Hoping not to wake her son, her voice dropped to an outraged whisper. "This is my home and that is my baby. I demand to know what you're doing."

He stood over the crib, his hands on the side rail examining the sleeping infant.

Carrie fiddled with Benny's blanket, her hands hovering protectively over her baby.

Aaron walked to the closet, opened the door, and checked the dark depths before closing it.

Shocked by his audacity, Carrie followed him out of the room.

He stopped and pointed at a closed door. "What's in here?"

"The bathroom." She no longer whispered. Her voice vibrated with anger.

He opened the door and looked in before shutting it and moving on to the next closed door. With a hand on the knob, he raised an eyebrow in silent question.

"That's my bedroom. You stay out of—*oooooh*!"

He checked the dark interior of her closet. With economic motions, he went down on his stomach beside the bed and checked under it. "All clear."

Carrie braced her hands on her hips. "What do you mean, 'all clear'? You sound like a cop."

Something flashed in his dark brown eyes. He urged her into the hall. With a hand splayed between her shoulder blades, he pushed her toward the living room. "Military training."

She should have guessed. Her first clue? The haircut. But his training and haircut did not give him the right to invade her privacy. She whirled around. "You have no right barging in here and...and...." She sputtered, too angry to pull her thoughts together. "You have no right, Aaron!"

"I came home—"

"I heard you drive in ages ago." She plucked an empty baby bottle off the coffee table.

He frowned at the interruption. "I walked to the corner for ice cream. When I came back your doors were wide open." His voice sharpened. "You're being stalked. An open door is an invitation." He ran a hand over his bristly hair. "When I heard the crash, and you screamed—"

"In case you hadn't noticed, it's hot and stinky in here!" She gestured with the bottle. "A skunk—"

"May have saved your life." His vehement words hung in the air.

Tears prickled behind Carrie's eyes. "What do you mean?"

The hard planes of his face softened a fraction. Some of the tension drained out of him. "Don't cry." He stepped closer, his eyes no longer remote and fierce.

"I can't help it." She blinked. "What about the skunk?"

He hesitated, and then as if coming to a decision, he spoke. "Someone was sneaking around outside your apartment."

Carrie swayed.

Aaron caught her by the shoulders and eased her into the

big chair. He squatted on his heels in front of her, his brow knit in concern. "You gonna faint on me?"

She shook her head. "Someone was out there?" Her mind churned along at the speed of a slug.

"I wouldn't have let him hurt you."

Her eyes filled again with tears. She felt protected and safe, which was silly because she barely knew this man. "So what happened?"

His lips tipped in a wry grin. "A skunk beat me to him. The guy climbed your back steps, not knowing the animal was underneath them."

"I was putting Benny to bed and thought I heard a noise, but I got distracted by the smell."

"Pretty foul, huh?"

Nodding she fell silent, staring at her hands clasped together in her lap. Sneaking around wasn't Ross's style. Who, then? "Thank God for the skunk." The words startled her into realization. "A skunk!" She looked at Aaron hunkered down in front of her.

"Yeah?" He hitched back a fraction, his expression uncertain.

"I don't think I've ever had a skunk under my step."

He frowned. "Not sure how you'd know, but one showed up tonight."

"Yes, it did." She wiped at the tears running down her cheeks and forced her voice around the lump in her throat. "It was another miracle."

Aaron cleared his throat. "I call it a coincidence."

She couldn't hold back the breathy giggle that filled her chest. "Of course you would. But with God there are no coincidences."

"Are you saying God used a skunk? To do what? Keep a bad guy away?"

"He did tonight." Certainty filled her with joy and confidence. Her God could do *anything*.

"Okay, so call me a skeptic." He stood up. "But whatever happened to God using angels?"

Carrie bounced off the chair after him. "I don't know. Maybe He saves them for the big stuff."

His eyes, so dark she could get lost in them, searched her face. "Your safety. Your life. That's big stuff, Carrie."

Her green eyes grew wide with surprise as the same feeling jolted through Aaron.

Exactly what corner of your brain did that pop out of, Black? Afraid she'd toss him out he walked into her kitchen and lifted the fan off the floor.

"You don't have to do that." She stood in the doorway, looking small and vulnerable.

"Don't want you hurting yourself again." He frowned. "Open windows are as much an invitation as open doors."

"If I close all the windows and doors, Benny and I will suffocate in heat, not to mention the stink."

She was right, but that didn't change the fact she was in danger. He wrestled the fan into the window and twisted the knob to the low setting. "Please promise me you'll keep your doors closed."

"I will."

"And if you're afraid, holler for me."

"I'm fine." She dismissed his concern with a wave of her hand. "I'm not a nervous Nellie, and I don't plan on waking you over some imagined boogie man."

"I did *not* make this person up, and you haven't imagined being followed. Who is he?"

She clamped her lips tight.

"It's all very real and at some point you'll tell me everything." He stepped closer to the back door. "If you need me, shout."

"Where will you be?" she asked.

"Watching the house."

She frowned. "All night? Surely that person won't come back."

"Perhaps he's hoping that's exactly what we'll think."

"But when will you sleep?"

He shrugged and opened the door. "Lock this behind me." He stood on the top step.

Behind the thin fabric of the window curtain, her shadowy form walked to the door and pushed the dead bolt in place.

"Good night, Carrie."

Her head snapped up. She couldn't see him standing in the dark on the other side of the door, but he waited, hoping. And then he heard her.

"Good night, Aaron."

Retrieving the flashlight he kept stashed in the saddlebag on his bike, Aaron began a thorough inspection of the yard. He searched the hedge where the prowler crashed through but found nothing to help him identify the person. He'd check again in the morning. In the meantime, a long night stretched ahead of him. Coffee would help, but he'd been through other long nights without a stimulant to keep him going.

Restless, he walked the perimeter of the yard. As sure as he was of his own abilities he wouldn't mind help. He'd even accept the divine kind. He shook his head and snorted. All the talk about God and miracles was getting to him.

Carrie reminded him of his grandmother. He'd lived with her as a kid growing up. The woman had been a walking Bible. She could quote an appropriate verse no matter what the occasion. He recalled the last time he'd spoken to her, just before his unit was sent to South America to extract a diplomat who'd gotten himself into a heap of trouble.

The phone connection had been poor. He'd strained to hear her. As always, the first question out of her mouth was the same one she always asked. "Have you gone to church?" The answer to that question was "no." He wasn't praying anymore, either.

Aaron paused. Above the town only the brightest stars dotted the night sky, and beyond that, heaven. The anger he carried deep inside churned in his belly. Good men were lost on that mission. Everyone knew what they were walking into and still they went willingly. Where was God that day?

Carrie was so sure, so content in her belief in God and His ability to work miracles. She remained convinced He'd use something as lowly as a skunk to carry out His will.

Uncomfortable with his own thoughts, he half-heartedly murmured, "She believes in You. Don't disappoint her. You better not let anything happen to her." The belligerent prayer was the first one he'd said in a long time.

Carrie hurried through her shower before feeding and dressing Benny. Saturday mornings during the summer were always a rush. She liked to go to the yard sales early. Throughout her morning routine, she'd glanced out first one window and then another trying to catch a glimpse of Aaron. She never spotted him. Had he gotten too tired to hang around outside all night and gone to bed instead?

Her teakettle whistled. Settling Benny in his playpen, she poured hot water into a mug containing instant coffee crystals and went in search of Aaron.

Stepping out on the front porch, she almost tripped over his long legs. He sat sprawled in the old wicker chair, head leaning against the house. Soft snores vibrated from between his parted lips. Hoping not to wake him, she stepped back.

"That coffee?"

She jumped and nearly spilled the contents of the mug. "I didn't mean to wake you."

"'S'okay." A sleepy burr ran through his voice. He rubbed his face and yawned. "I sat down when I heard you moving around indoors."

"Did anyone come back?"

"No." He eyed the mug, and she held it out to him. "It's black. If you want milk and sugar I have some."

"This is fine. Thanks." He sipped, testing the heat.

"Thank you for staying up—just in case."

He gave a quick nod and took another swallow.

As she fiddled with the plastic bangle bracelets circling her wrist, the silence grew awkward. "I better get going."

Her words brought him out of his quiet contemplation. "You're going out?"

"I'm a yard sale early bird."

He stood up. "I'll go with you."

"But...but you should get some sleep."

"Do I have time to change?"

"No. I want to go now." Hurrying indoors, she berated herself for being so ungrateful. The man stayed up all night on her behalf. *Admit it, Carrie. You're attracted to him. And a man—any man—is not part of your plan. Been there, done that and not successfully.*

"Come on, sweetie pie." She lifted Benny from his playpen. Slinging his diaper bag over her shoulder, she locked up, stepped out onto the porch, and halted.

Aaron leaned against her car, coffee mug in hand.

This didn't look promising. "What are you waiting for?"

"Not what. Who. Give me your keys. I'm driving."

"You need sleep."

"If we stand here arguing, you'll miss the bargains." He held out his hand in silent demand.

He was right. She unzipped her waist pouch and handed over the keys.

Aaron absorbed space in the car like a sponge soaked up water. Determined to concentrate on the classifieds in the newspaper draped across her lap, and not on the muscular shoulder only inches away from her own, Carrie gave him directions to their first stop.

When they arrived, cars already lined both sides of the street. Aaron waited for her while she unloaded Benny. He walked with her up the private driveway between makeshift tables loaded with household odds and ends.

Carrie settled on a small picture book for Benny and handed a quarter to the stout woman wearing a carpenter's apron that jingled with coins.

"All set?" Munching on a freshly baked blueberry muffin he'd bought at another table, he took her purchase and carried it for her. His gaze lingered on Benny, but he didn't say anything more.

The next stop was an estate sale spread over the front lawn of an old Victorian house.

"A toaster!" Carrie made a beeline to the table.

"Does it work?" Aaron hefted the older model appliance. "Cord's okay. Handle's chipped."

The elderly homeowner approached with a yellow extension cord in hand. "Feel free to try it, folks."

Aaron plugged in the toaster, carrying on a conversation with the man. "Works fine. Do you have a fan?"

"Sure do. Powerful, too. Built it myself." The man

hobbled off and pulled a huge fan from beneath a table piled with household linens.

Carrie pressed her lips against Benny's soft brow to stifle a giggle. The ancient fan looked like something that belonged on the front of an airplane.

Aaron's eyes lit up as he plugged it in for a test run. He flipped the switch, and the blades whirred to life.

Crocheted doilies flew through the air like giant snowflakes being swept along by a strong nor'east wind.

"Turn it off!" Laughing, Carrie poked Aaron and pointed at the surprised shoppers being pelted with linens.

He flipped the switch apologizing.

Amid laughter and good-natured joking, shoppers helped gather the doilies and pile them on the table.

Aaron pulled out his wallet. "I'd like to take the fan and the toaster."

Carrie opened her mouth to protest his purchasing the toaster for her, but the old man cut her off.

"Put away your money and take 'em, son. I haven't laughed like that in ages. Besides, my Martha, God rest her soul, would have been happy to know a nice young family took our old toaster and fan. You take them with my blessing. And here," with crooked fingers, he tucked a doily in Aaron's t-shirt pocket. "That's for your pretty little wife."

The comment left Carrie momentarily speechless.

Aaron thanked the man and placed the toaster under his arm. Carrying the fan in his other hand, he set off for the car.

She hurried after him. "You didn't correct him, Aaron."

He loaded the toaster and fan into the car. "He made a harmless assumption."

"But incorrect."

He shrugged. "No harm done. He'll never see us again."

Carrie tucked Benny into his car seat before climbing in

to ride shotgun. She waited for Aaron to get in. "He doesn't know the truth."

Aaron focused his full attention on her.

His eyes burned into her, sending little quakes of trepidation along her spine.

"We're buying household stuff and you're holding a baby. You want me to tell him we aren't a family? That we're not married?"

"We aren't!"

"And what do you suppose he'll think? That I'm not man enough to marry the mother of my kid?" Aaron blew out an irritated breath. "To be honest, I'm not even part of the equation. Should I say that you—" He twisted away and watched shoppers hustle past the car.

Carrie's stomach hurt. She wrapped her arms across her midriff. "That I what?"

He gripped the steering wheel so hard his knuckles turned white. "I don't know. Because I don't know the truth either, Carrie." He started the car. "Where to next?"

The newspaper page was marked with a half dozen red circles. They blurred, and she blinked back the threatening tears. "Home. Let's go home."

His jaw tightened. "I said I'd take you around, and I will. Tell me where you want to go."

"I found my toaster. That's enough for today." She tried to appear unaffected by his words but failed miserably. Swamped with an emotion she couldn't define, hurting deep inside, she needed time to think. And cry. "Please, take me home."

Chapter Six

Aaron set the fan at the bottom of the stairs and carried the diaper bag and toaster into Carrie's apartment. "Are you staying home?"

She nodded, afraid if she tried to speak she'd burst into tears.

"Good. I'm going to bed." He stepped toward the door and stopped. "If anyone you don't know comes to the door, don't answer it." Not waiting for her to respond, he stepped into the foyer. "Since we're both in, I'm locking the front entry door. Come get me if you need me."

Carrie listened to him secure the house and climb the stairs to his apartment. Pressing her lips against Benny's sweetly scented shoulder, she suppressed the sob lodged in her throat. She would not cry. If Aaron heard her, he'd come to investigate and demand an explanation she was incapable of giving him.

Thankful for her son's easygoing temperament, Carrie settled into her rocker to feed him his midmorning bottle. She closed her eyes to pray, but her thoughts swung wildly between last night and this morning. Drowning in emotions that were too close to the surface, Carrie fought to hold off the tears that threatened. Perhaps talking to Thelma would help.

She blotted Benny's moist lips and changed his diaper. Hooking the ever-present diaper bag over her arm, she let herself out the back kitchen door and walked to the little cottage. She rapped lightly on the purple door. "Aunt Thelma?"

"Come in, dear." Thelma's welcoming smile faltered. "What's wrong?"

Carrie shook her head, unable to speak. She followed Thelma into the small parlor.

"Did you go to the yard sales this morning?"

"Yes. Aaron drove." Carrie surrendered the baby to her friend and sat in a rocker matching the one Thelma settled into. Only the rhythmic squeak of wood broke the quiet. "Aaron saw someone lurking in our yard last night." She tried to minimize the danger and maximize Aaron's handling of the situation.

"Call the police." Thelma rocked faster, patting and stroking the baby sleeping on her shoulder.

The disturbing episode wasn't what had Carrie in an emotional quagmire. "Aaron stayed awake all night to be sure the man didn't come back." She fidgeted with her bright bracelets, clicking them one by one up and down her forearm. "Why is he so nice to me?"

Gentle laughter hedged Thelma's voice. "You're an attractive young woman."

"With a baby." Carrie paused. "He has no idea what I've gone through."

"So tell him."

She shifted uncomfortable. "It won't matter to him."

"Are you sure?" Thelma's eyes sparkled and the corners of her lips turned up.

Feeling like a sulky three year old, Carrie wanted to stick out her bottom lip and have a good pout. What would Aaron think of her if she told him? *Coward,* a little voice in her head taunted. She ignored the voice and plowed on. "He says he's given up on God."

"Oh dear." Thelma's pat-patting on Benny's back picked up-tempo. "Did he say why?"

"No." *Secrets.* Carrie played with the ruffled hem of her cotton top. She knew all about secrets. "And he's afraid of babies."

Thelma *tsked* and rocked faster. "Perhaps he's never been around them."

Carrie shrugged. He hadn't been tentative about holding Benny. He'd been scared. After seeing him handle last night's episode with the prowler, the man didn't scare easily.

Thelma's head bobbed in time with her rocking and patting Benny. "Perhaps that young man needs you and Benny as much as you need him."

"But I don't *want* to need him." Carrie's voice wobbled. She pushed the floor with her feet, rocking back and forth, soon out-pacing Thelma. "He's so big and…dominant."

"Has he done anything to frighten you?" Concern wove through Thelma's question.

"No." Carrie's voice raised an octave. "Just the opposite. I feel safe with him." And she did, except for that one time when he cornered her in the chair. As soon as he realized he'd scared her, he backed off. "It would be so easy to let him take charge." Swallowing a sob, she rushed on. "I won't trust another man." The sob escaped. She took shallow breaths between words. "Especially. One. That. Orders. Me. Around."

The floodgates opened releasing a gush of tears. She managed to take a breath only to have the air forced from her lungs in another gut-wrenching sob.

Thelma placed a box of facial tissues on her lap.

Pulling out one after another, Carrie wiped at her eyes and blew her nose. The tears continued and soon a pile of wet, wadded-up tissues filled her lap. Her eyes burned. Her nose stung. Her chest and stomach muscles ached.

Thelma patted her hand. "There's a difference between a man wanting to control you and a man expressing true concern for you."

Physically weary and emotionally spent, Carrie leaned back in the chair. She couldn't keep her eyes open. Tears continued to flow from beneath her swollen lids. The creak of rockers and the occasional sigh from Benny broke the heavy silence.

Carrie awoke to find the chair beside her empty. Her conversation with Thelma came crashing back. Her attraction to Aaron frightened her. She didn't want to make another mistake. "Lord, you know I don't want to count on anyone to take care of Benny and me." She sighed. "But if I'm supposed to let *someone* help us, give me the wisdom to accept the help." She tacked on a quick "amen" hoping God paid attention to unenthusiastic prayers.

Thelma was in the bedroom creating a cozy nest in the middle of her bed for Benny. Holding a gnarled finger to her lips, she tiptoed from the room. "I could use a cup of tea. How about you?"

Rubbing the last of the sleep from her eyes, Carrie followed her friend into the kitchen. She sank onto the vinyl seat of the circa 1950 kitchen set.

The ritual of making tea and the warmth of the drink soothed Carrie.

Lingering over steaming cups, she heard quick footsteps thump across Thelma's porch. The front door shook beneath a heavy pounding.

"Thelma?" The loud voice was unmistakable.

Thelma hurried to let Aaron in. "What's happened?"

"Have you seen Carrie?" He stepped inside and grasped both of Thelma's shoulders. "She's not in her—"

"I'm right here." Little shivers danced over Carrie's skin.

He shot a brief glance her way without comprehension, only to whip around a moment later, his gaze hard.

Her heart stuttered, and she took a step back. "I'm here."

"You said you were staying in." He let go of Thelma and faced her.

Carrie crossed her arms. She wasn't a child to be reprimanded. "I needed to talk to Thelma."

He stood ridged in the open door, his gaze boring into her. "You've been crying. What happened? You should have come to me."

She lifted her chin. "You couldn't help me with this."

"How do you know? You didn't give me a chance to try." His jaw clenched. "Did you receive another call?"

"No. And even if I did, you can't protect me every second of the day."

"Ahem." Thelma's grin deepened the creases in her aged face. "I'll check on Benny." She bustled away, merrily humming to herself.

To stop his hands from shaking, Aaron crossed his arms and jammed his fists into his armpits. This woman turned him inside out. "Next time you go out," he couldn't help but glare at her, "at least leave me a note in the hall."

"I don't answer to you."

He refused to be dragged into a fight. She'd already gone eight rounds with a box of tissues. Her skin was blotchy, her nose bright red, and her eyes mere slits. "Gonna tell me why you're crying?"

She balled the tissue in her hand and shook her head.

Frustrated, he said, "Get Benny ready to go. I'll come back in a few minutes to take you home."

Her head snapped up. "Where are you going?"

"Out to check the yard." He spun around to leave and a shiver raced up his spine. He'd forgotten the door behind him stood open leaving his back exposed. Placing the blame for his carelessness squarely on his obsession over an obstinate little redhead, he ducked outside before he did something stupid like hug her until the fear making his heart race dissipated. To follow through on that urge would only send his heart rate skyrocketing for a different reason.

Aaron followed Carrie into her apartment prepared to press her for more answers. He hadn't discovered anything new in the yard, but his gut insisted time was running out.

"Who is he, Carrie?" He set the diaper bag on the floor.

She kissed Benny's fuzzy crown and placed him in the playpen. Without so much as a glance Aaron's way, she walked into the kitchen to prepare lunch.

He followed. "I'm not going away so you may as well talk. Who is this creep? What does he want?" The sour taste of fear lingered on his tongue.

She stood at the sink washing her hands. The sun streaming through the window glinted off her hair.

He fisted his hands at his sides, struggling to keep from reaching out and stroking the fiery strands.

"I don't know." She refused to meet his gaze.

He handed her a towel.

She grasped the end, but instead of letting go, he held on causing her to glance at him. "You're lying."

Her gaze skittered away.

Ha! Gotcha. He tugged on the cloth. "Isn't one of the Ten Commandments, 'Thou shalt not lie?'"

"No." She dropped her end of the towel. "That's not one of them." She marched over to the refrigerator.

Well, lookee there. The Ten Commandments were posted on the door of the fridge. He tossed the towel on the counter and stepped closer.

She ran her finger down a list held in place by small white beach stones backed with magnets.

He leaned close to read the list. "Bearing false witness." He straightened up. "Close enough."

She faced him, arms crossed over her soft curves. Her lemony scent teased him, and he couldn't resist the urge to touch her. He hooked a wayward strand of red-gold hair around his finger. Before she could slip away, he braced his other hand on the smooth cold enamel of the refrigerator trapping her. "Tell me who he is."

Eyes wide, she licked her rose pink lips.

He bit back a groan and leaned closer, seeking the warmth radiating from her. "Tell me."

"Benny's father."

He went still. Here it was. The question he hadn't asked. He let her hair slip from his finger as he stepped back. "Who *is* Benny's father?" He tried to keep the edge out of his voice.

She rummaged through the drawer of the small desk beside the fridge. "It's a long story." Finding a ponytail holder, she smoothed her hair away from her face and secured it.

He dropped into a kitchen chair. "I have all afternoon."

Feeling his eyes bore into her, Carrie pulled a wedge of cheese, bread, and butter from the refrigerator. "He's a man I met two years ago." She didn't want to explain the whole sorry affair to Aaron. The tale exposed too much of herself.

His long legs were stretched out and crossed at the ankles, but the relaxed pose didn't fool her. He played with the edges of the lace doily in the center of the table while his keen gaze tracked her every move. "Where did you meet him?"

"At a wedding reception. I worked for a catering company." She pulled out a breadboard and griddle. "I served his table their dinner. Ross was funny and charming. He joked around about...stuff."

"What stuff?"

Carrie placed a slice of cheese between two pieces of buttered bread. "Does it matter?" She shrugged. "Just stuff." Sliding the sandwich onto the griddle, she turned the burner on low.

"Humor me. What 'stuff' did he joke about? Be honest with me." His low voice had a measured cadence as though he was trying to stay calm.

She glared at him before furiously assembling another sandwich. "He complained the coffee was too hot." The heat of a blush climbed her neck and spread over her cheeks. "After that his comments got personal."

"How personal?"

She dropped the butter knife with a clatter and clung to the counter. "For heaven's sake, Aaron. Don't make me spell out every little thing. Personal enough I eventually had his child." A single tear burned down her already hot cheek.

He was on his feet in an instant, gathering her close in his arms. She wanted to push him away, but his hand gently glided across her shoulders, and his lips skimmed a warm trail across her temple. She stiffened her knees to keep from melting into his embrace.

"So what happened? Why aren't you with him any longer?"

The deep rumble of his voice brought Carrie back to earth. *What was she doing?* With every desire inside her crying to stay in his arms, she pulled away. She whirled about and sprinted for her front door. Desperation in her voice, she said, "You better go."

Hot on her heels, Aaron caught the ponytail holder as it slipped from her hair. He wanted to hold her again.

She yanked the door open and stepped aside.

He wished he could tell her everything would be fine, but he never made a promise he couldn't keep. "This conversation isn't over."

He stepped into the foyer. Behind him, the door slammed. Taking the stairs two at a time, he berated himself for not handling the situation better. He stormed into his kitchen and tossed the braided pink elastic on the table, adding it to his growing collection.

Funny and charming.

No one had ever described him as funny and charming. He needed a long ride on his bike. That's where he did his best thinking, but he didn't dare leave the house. The stubborn woman might not want his protection, but she was stuck with him.

The buzz of his phone jerked him out of his dark thoughts. He yanked it from his pocket and read the screen. Jason Cooper, his partner on the police force. "Yeah."

"Whoa, man. Whatever happened, I didn't do it."

"Hey, Jase." Aaron massaged his temple and paced between the kitchen and living room.

"Where are you?" The question was clipped and to the point.

"Rhode Island."

"Why there?"

Aaron didn't like being on the receiving end of all the questions a cop asked. "Because I couldn't go any farther without drowning."

"Chief says you haven't reported in."

"I'm on my own time." Aaron didn't try to keep the growl out of his voice. "You know what you can tell Chief Brady."

"Why don't you call and tell him yourself?" The pause that followed was heavy with unspoken thoughts. "Understand you haven't checked in with the doc either."

"And I don't plan to." Aaron blew out a long breath. He didn't want to discuss this right now.

"Part of the deal is talking to the shrink."

Anger hissed through Aaron. "What are you saying? No more counseling, no more partners?" They'd known each other for a long time. Would his best friend and partner on the force desert him?

The voice in his ear was low and measured. "I'll take you covering my back even on your worst day, Black. You're not doing this for *me*."

An image of Carrie blasted to the forefront of Aaron's thoughts. He flopped onto the couch.

"You still with me?" Jason's voice snapped Aaron's attention back to the conversation.

"Yeah, I'm here."

"You gonna tell me what's happening out there, or do I make the trip to see you?"

Aaron's chest tightened. He could trust Jason. "I have a situation here."

"I'm listening."

"The woman who lives below me has a stalker." Aaron sat forward and rested his elbows on his knees. "Ex-boyfriend."

"Tell me about the woman."

Aaron groaned. His partner could read him like a book. "Never mind that. His actions are escalating."

"What are the local police doing?"

Aaron blew out a breath, wishing he hadn't started this conversation. "They don't know about her problem. She's afraid of them."

"She got a name?"

"Carrie."

"Let me guess." Jason's voice had a wry twist to it. "Carrie doesn't know her neighbor is a cop from Chicago."

Aaron took a deep breath. "Get's better." He paused before the words come out in a rush. "She has a baby." He jerked the phone away from his ear to save his hearing as Jase let loose a string of cuss words. After a moment of quiet Aaron asked, "You finished?"

"I ought to come out there and pound some sense into that thick head of yours. Stop playing the hero."

He ignored the threat. "I may need your help."

"Whatever you want, you got it."

"Thanks." They talked a few more minutes, and he caved to Jason's demand to at least know his address.

"You better call me real soon with an update, or I'll come hunting you, you hear?" Jason didn't wait for an answer. The connection went dead.

Chapter Seven

An early Sunday morning hush blanketed the neighborhood. Aaron sipped his iced coffee. Today was gonna be another hot one. Resting his foot on the bottom step of the kitchen stoop, he leaned against the rail. "So tell me about Benny's father."

Dressed for church, Carrie stood on the top step watering potted flowers and pinching dead blossoms. Benny lounged in his carrier on the picnic table babbling and waving his pudgy hands at something only he could see.

The "funny and charming" comment about the old boyfriend still rankled. He'd spent most of the evening trying to figure out how she'd tag him. Not that it mattered.

"I'm leaving for church soon." She avoided eye contact with him.

He wanted more than anything to see her vivid green eyes. "That's why I'm here. I'm driving." *Yeah.* That got her attention.

Her eyes raked the length of him. "You're not dressed for church."

His only suit hung in his closet back in Chicago. "I'm chauffeuring."

She came down the steps in those ridiculous pink pointy-toed shoes of hers. A light breeze puffed the full skirt of her pastel floral dress and played with the tendrils of hair about her face. "Come to the service with us."

"Us?"

"Thelma and me." She stared at him, nibbling her bottom lip.

He wished he were the one doing the nibbling. Taking the watering can from her, he held it beneath the spigot. The thunder of water into the old tin container prevented him from having to answer her, thank God. *Ha!* He hadn't thanked God for anything in a long time. He turned off the faucet. "The church will fall on our heads if I step through the door."

She rolled her eyes. "Not likely." Taking the can from him, she sprinkled water on a small patch of flowers near the foundation of the house.

An uncomfortable silence wrapped around them like thick cotton. Her small hands caressed the bright red blossoms, and he had the foolish urge to lie in the muddy soil right along side the petunias. When she spoke, her voice was whisper thin.

"He came home drunk again."

Stillness spread through Aaron. He stood unmoving, letting her continue at her own pace.

"He's a mean drunk. Usually he inflicts his hurt with words." She paused and with a delicate touch, ran her fingers along a stalk of blue flowers. "But that night...." She shook her head. "Earlier that evening he got angry with me."

The deadly calm inside Aaron began to slip away.

"He hit...." She gulped, not finishing the sentence.

Aaron couldn't stop reaching for her any more than he could have not taken his next breath. He pulled her upright.

Taking the heavy can from her, he set it at their feet. Then she was in his arms, leaning against him, her breathing choppy. He was afraid to say anything. Afraid he'd say the wrong thing.

Burying his fingers in the hair at her nape, he fought back the seething anger at the man who dared to hurt her. The man who was funny and charming but only when he was sober.

His shoulder muffled her next words. "I was pregnant. I didn't want my baby hurt. So I left."

He rested his lips on top of her fiery head, fighting the urge to ask all the questions a cop asks. Instead he concentrated on how she fit perfectly beneath his chin.

"Carrie!" Thelma's call had the same effect as a blast of dynamite, shattering the moment into a hundred irretrievable little pieces.

They sprang apart.

Carrie spun away, leaving him edgy and wanting to pull her back into his arms.

Thank you, God, for Thelma and her nonstop chatter. For the second time in less than an hour, Aaron found himself talking to God. Funny how church people could compel a person to think about the Almighty. Thelma was filling the car with talk about recipes, church suppers, and babies. For all the old woman's effort at conversation, Aaron barely managed a civil "yes" or "no" when appropriate. He hadn't heard much more than that from Carrie.

Did she regret sharing her bad experience? Problem was he still didn't have the creep's name. Get that and he'd ask Jason to run a background check.

They pulled into the gravel church driveway as the peal of bells split the air calling the faithful to worship. Painted white and topped with a tall steeple, the church sat on a knoll. A stone wall ran along the edge of the parking lot. On the other side of the wall a large cemetery with neat rows of headstones and monuments climbed the hill in a series of tiers.

A family crossed the driveway. A tall man carried a little girl. She wore a sparkly crown that flashed in the morning sunlight. At his side, a pretty blonde woman did her best to keep two older girls moving.

He'd never experience what that man had. Stopping the car at the side entrance, Aaron helped Carrie and Thelma out.

"You sure you won't come in?" Carrie adjusted Benny's little hat. "No one cares how you're dressed."

His disreputable black jeans were his oldest pair and therefore the most comfortable. "Nah. Go ahead in." He fiddled with the radio knob.

"Are you going to wait here?" She handed Thelma the diaper bag.

"Nope. Your gauge is almost on empty. I'll go gas up for you."

She blushed. "You don't have to do that."

"Go on in. I'll be here when you're ready to leave."

Hands full, Carrie and Thelma entered the church.

The pang of loneliness in his chest was a foreign sensation. "Get a hold of yourself, Black," he muttered. He put the car in gear and pulled away from the church.

The streets were lively with traffic when Aaron stopped at the gas station. From now on he'd keep an eye on the gas gauge for her. He shuddered to think of Carrie and Benny stuck on the side of the road.

He filled the tank and checked the oil. Judging by the amount of fine sand on the floor of the car, Carrie went to the beach often. He had time to kill so he pulled around behind the station to the car vacuum. Like a sleeping dragon, a huge black and chrome car vac sat on the edge of the lot hemmed in by protective steel posts.

Collecting the clutter he stashed stray pennies, a baby rattle, and other small odds and ends into the glove compartment. The yellow ponytail holder he found between the seat and the center console went straight into his pocket.

He fed quarters into the machine and flipped the switch. The vacuum whined to life, inhaling with a steady deafening drone. The wide plastic hose he held vibrated and writhed. He leaned into the passenger side and shoved the long black wand under the seat. Sand hissed through the hose followed by a loud clatter. He yanked the wand out and bent over to peer under the front seat.

A sharp burst of pain exploded over the back of his head. The rough carpet burned his cheek. Then everything went black.

"Bye, Auntie." Carrie waved at Thelma and her friend, Pauline, as they left the nursery. The older ladies had decided last minute to go for lunch and were debating the merits of the fast food restaurants close by. Pauline planned to drive Thelma home after their meal.

Stuffing her Bible in the diaper bag, Carrie checked Benny's diaper before lifting him to her shoulder. As usual, she was the last one to leave the church nursery. She enjoyed the fellowship of the other young mothers and the occasional grandmother that gravitated to the cries of a baby.

Hiking the diaper bag to her shoulder, Carrie hurried down the hall. Her stomach gave a funny little lurch. Aaron should be waiting for her at the side entrance. She'd been awake half the night thinking about him, wondering if she'd done the right thing making him leave yesterday.

She stepped out onto the flagstone terrace. The parking lot was empty except for Mr. Beedle's ancient jalopy. Sighing, she settled on the bench beside the door where a small overhang protected her from the sun. Anticipation warred with relief that Aaron hadn't arrived yet.

The church door opened and Mr. Beedle stuck his head out. His bushy gray eyebrows banged together over the bridge of his nose. "Do you have a ride home, young lady? I'm locking up."

"Yes. I have a ride coming."

The old man harrumphed and jiggled the door handle. "If you're here when I finish up, I'll take you home myself." He went back inside, the door closing behind him.

Carrie smiled. She'd never seen Mr. Beedle in a suit. Sunday was his busiest day.

Benny took his fist out of his mouth and reached for her hair. He tangled his fingers in the thick locks and pulled.

"Ow, you!" Making a face, Carrie untangled her hair from his wet grip. "You're getting strong, tough guy." She smooched his fat cheek with a noisy kiss. "Give me a minute." She pulled a flannel pad from the diaper bag and bent to spread it on the flagstones before laying Benny on his back. Fishing in the small pockets that lined the bag, she found a wide stretchy ponytail holder fashioned of little pearl beads. She gathered up her hair. "Won't stay in long." She picked Benny up. "We both know that, don't we?"

Tires crunched on the gravel drive of the church.

Expecting to see her car with Aaron behind the wheel, a

tremor of fear raced through Carrie at the sight of the black SUV approaching. She lunged to her feet. *God, where is Aaron?* Side stepping to the church door, she grabbed the handle. The thumb latch didn't budge. Desperate, she shook the door rattling the windowpanes. "Mr. Beedle?"

The SUV was closer.

Clutching Benny to her chest, Carrie stumbled across the drive unsteady on her heels. One foot rolled to the side twisting her ankle. She kicked off that shoe and lurched with an uneven gait through the gap in the stone wall that allowed cars to enter the cemetery. Using precious seconds, she stopped to kick off the other shoe. Stones ground against the soles of her feet before she was able to leap onto the grass.

She ran up a small rise, darting between headstones and across graves. Benny squalled, unhappy with the rough handling. Sweeping her hair from her eyes, she headed toward the other side of the cemetery and the fast food joint where Thelma and Pauline were eating lunch.

She glanced back. The SUV entered the cemetery and followed the narrow lane zigzagging up the hill. Ducking behind the column of a small Greek pavilion, Carrie leaned against the cool granite, gasping for breath. Fear rolled through her in waves. Unhappy and hungry, Benny cried harder. No amount of rocking or shushing quieted him.

She peeked out around the column. She didn't see any sign of the vehicle, though she did hear the purr of an engine. Tears blurred her vision. She dashed them away. Adjusting her grip on Benny, she left the shadow of the tomb staying close to the ground.

The purr of the engine grew louder.

She bolted from one large headstone to the next. She peeked from behind a large obelisk and saw the SUV stopped on the tier above her.

The vehicle changed direction, causing Carrie to double back. Loud sobs wrenched from her burning lungs. She bent to one side trying to ease a stitch in her diaphragm. Staggering over uneven ground, she ignored the pain in her ankle. Tears streamed down her face and a desperate prayer whirled round in her head. *God, please, send me help. I need Aaron.*

A giant sucking leech gripped Aaron by the throat. He wrapped his hand around a shuddering tube and pulled, finding instant relief. Fighting the black mist threatening to engulf him, a sense of urgency pressed in. The loud moan of a machine deafened him. He opened his eyes, willing away the constant jabbing pain in his head.

The odor of musty carpet penetrated his senses. Using his hands for leverage he rose and banged the back of his head. Excruciating pain sent him to the carpet. He swallowed the bile rising in the back of his throat.

He was wedged into a small space, though his legs had room to move. Taking care, he inched back until his knees hit a hard surface. Lifting his head, a stick shift came into his line of vision.

A sudden flood of memories pounded through his brain. He was in Carrie's car. He'd been cleaning it for her. He gingerly probed the sore lump on his head as he scrambled to his feet. The bright sunlight hurt his eyes.

He was late for Carrie and Thelma.

Aaron's heart rate spiked, increasing the pounding pain in his injured head. The Sunday drivers in town were out for their weekly gawk and dawdle. He laid on the horn when one driver rode the brakes at 25 mph. on a straight stretch.

He passed the car on the double yellow lines. If the cops wanted to ticket him they'd have to do it in the churchyard.

No sirens or flashing lights showed up in his rearview mirror so he pushed harder and faster. His gut knotted. Now would be a good time to pray.

An elderly man drove out in front of him. He bit back a sharp oath. God probably wouldn't listen to a prayer uttered in the same breath as a few choice swear words. And he needed God to listen.

"Okay, here's the deal, God. Carrie may be in trouble." He paused. "You probably know that. Keep her safe till I get there. And if You want to stick around and help out that's okay, too. Well, that's all. So, amen."

He gunned the motor, skidding into the church driveway, spraying gravel with his tires as he sped up the knoll. Fear raced along his spine. The only vehicle in the parking lot was an old Dodge truck.

He stopped the car across three parking spaces and lunged out, running to the church door where he'd left Carrie and Thelma earlier. The sight of Benny's diaper bag abandoned on the flagstone caused spears of hot and cold to tear through his chest.

"Carrie?" He pulled on the door handle. The door held fast. He shook it and bellowed, pounding on the wood with his fist until a windowpane popped free of the glazing and fell with a splintering crash to the step.

A dark silhouette inside walked closer. As the person neared the door, the light streaming in through the window revealed an elderly man with a thick shock of gray hair sticking straight up.

Aaron spoke through the broken window as the old man fumbled to unlock the door. "Where's Carrie?"

The man's khakis were neat but frayed, and the name

"Beedle" was stitched over the breast pocket. Eyes sharp, he stepped out the door. "She was right here."

"Did she go inside?"

"No, I was locking up."

This time Aaron didn't bother to stop the pungent remarks from flying off his tongue. He scanned the drive. A spot of pink caught his eye, and he took off at a run.

Her shoe. The heel dangled by a nail.

The pain in his head was nothing compared to the hurt ripping through his heart. She'd been running. *God help her.* She'd keep running straight to put distance between herself and the danger.

He ran across the second shoe on the other side of the stone wall. A bright beacon cast off on the crushed stone that crunched beneath his boots. She was barefoot and couldn't stay on the rocks. He quartered the area with his gaze, searching for a clue.

In the distance, a motor rumbled.

He jogged to the crest of a knoll. Below were row upon row of headstones with the occasional small American flag. Something white gleamed in the grass nearby, and he went to investigate.

A ponytail holder.

He scooped it up. On the run, he worked the beaded elastic onto his wrist. He ignored the pain each pounding footstep sent straight to his aching head. She had to be here. And the baby. *Lord watch over Benny, too.*

Reaching the summit of the small rise, the sight below triggered a gut-wrenching explosion that rocked him to his core.

Benny's shrill cries rent the air as Carrie stumbled between headstones and monuments. A black SUV pursued her in a dangerous game of cat and mouse.

Aaron hunched low, tracking the movement of the vehicle. "Game over, fur ball. That sweet little mousy is mine."

Chapter Eight

Disoriented, Carrie crouched low next to a white marble monument. Tears streamed down her cheeks. Sobs tore at her chest. She'd lost all sense of direction in the chase.

A motor revved, coming closer.

She scrambled from her hiding place and ran blindly, clutching Benny close to her pounding heart. Her foot caught in a dip in the turf. A terrible pain shot through her ankle. Falling, she twisted her body to keep from landing on top of Benny. Her knees and elbow burned from the impact.

Terror brought her to her feet. She plunged past a wide headstone, screaming when a strong arm closed around her waist, yanking her backwards against a hard immovable wall.

"Noooo." She fought to break free.

"Hush, sweetheart. It's me."

Carrie froze, afraid to believe she recognized the deep voice close to her ear.

"I've got you."

"Aaron?" The arm circling her waist had a beaded ponytail holder wrapped around the thick wrist.

"Yeah."

She tipped her head back. "Thank you, God." Safe in his arms, she leaned against him and fought to catch her breath. Nearby she heard the grate of tires against gravel. A tremor rocked through her, and he gave her a tight reassuring squeeze.

"Can you quiet the baby?" Aaron's soft voice was at complete odds with the tension radiating from him.

Carrie nestled Benny closer.

"Is that Ross following you?"

She nodded.

He scrutinized the area. "See the angel on the top of the hill? Do you have the strength to climb?"

She nodded. She had no choice.

"Come on then. Keep low." He pulled her snug against his side. Wrapping an arm around her, he pressed his other hand over hers as she held Benny against her shoulder.

The thick grass brushed the bruised soles of her feet. Her ankle hurt and her knees threatened to buckle as she lurched along beside him. When he stopped beside a gray granite headstone adorned with lilies and butterflies, she sank to her knees. He crouched next to her, stroking her back.

Aaron tracked the course of the SUV. Ross stuck to the gravel lanes, never veering off to run across the gravesites. Aaron respected the dead, but his first concern was protecting the living. He'd run across every grave in the cemetery if that meant keeping Carrie and Benny safe.

Beneath his hand, Carrie's back rose and fell as she labored to catch her breath. The sole of one bare foot peeped from beneath the hem of her dress. Cuts and scratches marked it. Anger burned through him. Anger at Mr. Funny and Charming. And anger at himself for not being with her when she most needed him.

Benny let out another wail.

Carrie couldn't climb the hill and carry the baby, too. She was running on nothing but willpower. Shutting down the fear clawing at his chest, Aaron reached for the baby. "Give him to me." The words were harsh and clipped, but he feared he'd change his mind if he took the time to think.

"What?" A haze of doubt clouded her eyes.

"The baby. Give him to me." He held out his hands and hoped she didn't see the slight tremor. Prepared for her rejection, ready to force the issue if necessary, she surprised him when she surrendered Benny. She was in worse shape than he'd thought.

His gut flipped. *Lord, don't let me drop him.* The desperate plea cranked around in his head as he cradled the baby in his arms.

Silence dropped like a curtain.

Benny spread his little mouth in a huge yawn and his eyes drifted shut. Alarmed, Aaron looked at Carrie. "What'd I do?" Her breathless giggle didn't help him.

"He feels safe with you."

His heart hammered double time. *The kid is clueless. So is his mother.*

The hum of a motor grew louder.

Hands shaking, Aaron snugged the baby into the crook of his arm before taking Carrie's hand. "C'mon. Let's go." Trained to focus on the situation at hand, he didn't allow his mind to wander to the warmth of Carrie's hand in his or the child he held.

The ascent to the crest of the hill involved climbing a series of tiers while the SUV followed the *zigzag* curves of the laneway to reach the top terrace and the angel statue. His hoped to arrive at the top before the SUV, then make a rapid descent on the opposite side to the street and the businesses below.

Digging in with the toes of his boots, he climbed each hump of sod to the next tier, hauling Carrie behind him. Her breath rasped in her throat and her features contorted in a mask of pain and terror.

"Just a little farther. You can do it."

Fear gave Carrie the momentum to keep going. Halfway up the last level, she stepped on the hem of her skirt and fell to her knees. Her cry of frustration ended in a squeak as Aaron clamped his arm around her rib cage and lifted her the last few steps.

Unceremoniously dumped on all fours, she pushed her hair off her face to look into the serene face of the seated stone angel.

Grasping one of the angel's huge toes, she struggled to her feet. But her ankle wouldn't support her. She crumbled and landed hard on her rear, jarring her backbone and rattling her teeth.

Aaron's harsh breath rasped in her ear. "Here." He thrust an oblivious Benny at her. Shoving one arm under her knees and wrapping the other around her back, he scooped her up as the sharp thump of a car door reverberated through the air. He whirled toward the sound so fast Carrie blinked to shake off vertigo and focus on the man charging up the hill.

"Does he own any weapons?"

"Not that I...*ooph*." She landed with a thump between two massive robed knees.

"Don't move." Aaron whipped around and stood with his feet braced wide to face Ross. "Carrie doesn't want anything to do with you."

"We have unfinished business." The sinister calm in Ross's voice indicated the extent of his anger. He pointed a finger at Carrie, anger burning in his eyes. "You left me. Nobody leaves me!" Ross stepped closer.

"Back off."

Aaron's guttural snarl stopped Ross's advance. His gaze snapped to the baby. "That's my kid."

The thud of Carrie's heart shook her whole body. She gripped Benny tighter as Ross moved nearer.

A boot scraped against gravel and Aaron bellowed with rage as he dove for the other man. Together they fell to the ground in a tangled, grunting heap of flying fists, arms, and legs.

Aaron rose on his knees and pinned Ross to the ground. His hand spanned Ross's throat. "You don't listen very well."

His face an ugly purple, Ross gasped for air. "She's mine." Using both fists he lashed out.

Aaron dodged them, grappling to regain his hold.

Benny wailed, and Ross's ruthless gaze locked on Carrie for a moment before darting upwards. He froze and then disbelief and fear and flitted across his face in fast succession.

Aaron shoved away from his opponent, remaining in a defensive crouch. "Get out of here. Now!"

Ross lurched to his feet. Breathing hard, he tore his eyes from whatever he was staring at overhead and shook his fist at Carrie. "Get rid of this guy or he's gonna get hurt. You hear me?" He slid down the incline and stumbled to his vehicle.

Her heart in her throat, Carrie watched Ross tear away in his car heedless of the sharp curves.

Aaron's face was a hard mask as he turned back to her. He took a step toward the angel monument where she crouched holding Benny and shaking uncontrollably.

A *pop pop* split the air. Aaron dropped to the grass.

"Aaron?" Carrie stepped from the protective cover of the statue. "Aaron, what…?"

In a blur, he shot to his feet and slammed her against the granite. His protective arm absorbed the brunt of the impact as he pressed her face against the hard wall of his chest. She rubbed her cheek against the hollow of his shoulder. Benny wiggled between them in protest.

"Wh-what happened?" Tears laced her voice.

"I duck when I'm shot at."

"You were shot?" Inside Carrie crumbled. She pushed at him, trying to see him, all of him. "Where? Show me."

"Hush a minute." Aaron tightened his grip on her as more pops punctuated the silence. He huffed a quiet laugh, finally recognizing the sound of an old vehicle backfiring. Relief washed over him in a wave so intense he felt light-headed. Of course, Carrie's hand running across his chest and down his side was pretty heady stuff, too. She tugged at his t-shirt, and he shackled her wrist with his hand. "What are you doing?"

"You said you were shot." Her voice seesawed.

"I'm not. I thought maybe, but I'm okay. Listen."

The clatter of metal and the hum and pop of an old engine grew louder.

"Somebody's coming." He wished she'd stop looking at

him with tears—and her heart—in her eyes. He focused on the old Dodge truck wending its way toward them. It was the same truck he'd seen in the church parking lot.

"Mr. Beedle." She pulled her arm from his grip. "The church custodian. His old jalopy makes that noise."

Aaron glanced toward the street lined with businesses. The brake lights of the SUV flashed before exiting the cemetery. "The old man has great timing. Kinda like the U.S. Cavalry coming to the rescue." His attempt to lighten the mood fell flat. Gathering Carrie and Benny into his arms, he leaned against the angel's knee to await Mr. Beedle's arrival.

Carrie shifted to look up at the stone angel looming above them. "Something scared Ross. He stared at the angel...."

Aaron groaned. *Not another one of her miracles.* Running his fingers up and down her arm, he wished she hadn't witnessed him going hand-to-hand with the ex-boyfriend.

The truck crash-jangled to a halt in front of them. The driver's door squealed, and Mr. Beedle stepped out. "Want a lift?"

His arm around Carrie, Aaron walked to the door the old man held open. "Yeah. Thanks." He set Carrie in the middle of the bench seat and squeezed his large frame in beside her. He'd need a can opener to get out. Settling one arm across the back of the seat, he placed his other hand on her pale forearm where she cradled Benny in her lap. After saving them from Ross whatever-his-last-name-was, Aaron wasn't about to let her and the baby fly through the windshield as they lurched and chugged their way to the church.

He leaned forward. "I'm sorry I broke the window."

The old man grunted.

Carrie's exhausted smile caused Aaron's heart to turn over—an odd sensation for a man who, until a few days ago was convinced he no longer had a heart.

The tip of her finger bumped across the wide ponytail holder on his wrist. "You found it."

Because there was no other way in such cramped quarters, he lifted both hands high over her head. The thing pinched and left him minus a few hairs as he pulled it off. Too bad he had to give it back. Faux pearls would have been a nice addition to his collection.

Mr. Beedle stopped next to Carrie's station wagon.

Aaron managed a less than graceful exit from the small cab.

Carrie brushed aside his help.

"I'm not a sack of potatoes." She scooted to the edge of the seat, clinging to Benny.

Stepping back, Aaron folded his arms across his chest. Grass and dirt stained her torn dress. Her hair flew wild. Her feet were cut and bruised, and her ankle was swollen. And she *still* had spunk enough to snap at him. "Don't drop the baby."

She sniffed and grasped the door handle. Legs extended, she slid off the seat—and didn't stop sinking. Aaron caught her and gently lowered her to the ground.

He squatted next to her. "You ready to let me carry you?" Her expression would've been comical if he hadn't understood the extent of her anger and humiliation.

At her curt little nod, he once again scooped her and Benny up. Soft and warm in his arms, he couldn't resist whispering, "Not in a million years could I mistake you for a bag of potatoes."

Her green eyes grew round before she ducked her head to hide her face from him.

She went into the car easily. He had a harder time securing Benny in his car seat. The problem wasn't the buckle. The monster called Fear kept his fingers from working properly.

"Here you go, young fella." Mr. Beedle passed Aaron the diaper bag.

"Thank you for the ride." Aaron extended his hand.

The custodian took it in a hard grip. "Nine o'clock tomorrow morning I'm repairing that window." His faded gray eyes bore into Aaron.

"Yes, sir. I'll be here to lend a hand."

Numb, Carrie leaned her head back on the car seat and closed her eyes, not opening them until Aaron drove the car into their driveway.

"Wait here while I check the house." He got out and climbed the steps with caution as if expecting more trouble.

She sighed and twisted in her seat to check Benny. "Hey, babykins. You doing okay?" She smoothed the shirt over his belly. "If Aaron hadn't come when he did—" Carrie bit her bottom lip and swallowed to keep the tears at bay.

Her door opened. Aaron squatted on his heels beside the car. "All good inside. How are you feeling?" He brushed dirt from the hem of her dress.

"Okay."

He quirked an eyebrow.

"Maybe not perfectly okay," she hedged. "But okay enough to walk into the house. I think." Her feet felt like a size twelve and pulsed with pain.

He shook his head and stood to open the rear car door. A moment later he placed Benny in her lap. Before she could protest, he lifted her out of the car.

Airborne for the third time today, Carrie sighed and rested her head against his shoulder.

Settled on her couch with Benny at her side, not until

Aaron came in for a second time carrying the diaper bag did she remember she hadn't given him a key to her door. "How did you get into my apartment?"

One corner of his mouth tipped up. "One of your miracles, maybe?" He strode into her kitchen and out of sight.

"For your information I think another miracle *did* happen." In the kitchen, cupboard doors were opening and closing and water was running. "Ross saw something that frightened him. Something about the angel."

Aaron stepped through the doorway, a steaming stockpot in his hands and a dishtowel slung over his shoulder. "From what I recall of Sunday school eons ago, everyone present knew when a miracle occurred." He knelt in front of her and set the pot on the rug. A heavy layer of bubbles floated on top of the water.

"What did you put in there?" Carrie swished her hand in the water to check the heat.

"The antibacterial hand soap next to the sink. Give me your foot."

"I cook in this pot."

"And right now, you're gonna soak your feet in it. Give me a foot."

She wanted to argue. The dishpan under the sink would have been a better choice. Too tired to fight she said, "My soup will never taste the same."

Chapter Nine

Aaron held her foot over the pan. Even swollen, it was small in his hand. He studied the tiny blue flowers decorating each hot pink nail. Scooping up a handful of soapy water, he tightened his grip when she hissed and tried to pull away.

"Too hot."

He shook his head, mesmerized by her wiggling toes. "Only feels that way. Hold still. When I finish, I'll pack that ankle with ice." Scooping up more water, he massaged her foot, taking care to gently rub the pad of each toe. This was crazy. He was crazy. He needed to get her out of his system. Somehow prove she was nothing special. A relationship was the last thing he wanted, especially if a baby was part of the deal.

He lowered her foot into the water and kneaded her heel. She drew in a breath. Her eyes were soft and warm. His mouth went dry and his hands stopped what they were doing. *One kiss.* Surely that would quench the inferno raging through him. He leaned forward and brushed his mouth across her petal soft lips.

Didn't help.

She was so deeply rooted in his heart more than one kiss was required. He brought his damp hand to the back of her head and held her still as he kissed her again, capturing her little gasp of breath and inhaling it as his own. Something he refused to name welled up in his chest. He groaned with the enormity of it.

A squirming fingertip and the sharp poke of a fingernail against his bottom lip cut through the haze enveloping his senses. He backed off a whisker. Her finger followed. "What're you doing?" he muttered, not ready to end what was happening between them.

"Stopping." Her breath whispered against his lips. Her eyes were unfocused and hazy.

"Don't want to."

"I know, but—"

He worked his way around the intruding finger and cut her off with another kiss. He heard her soft whimper just before she grasped both his ears and tugged. He rocked back. "What—"

She placed her hand over his mouth, accidentally poking his nose with his finger. "I'm not innocent, but chastity is important to me."

He couldn't help himself. He slanted a look at the baby sleeping next to her on the couch.

She sighed. "No matter what happened before, I want to be chaste now."

He smiled and nibbled on her fingers. "Then I'm your man. Chasing you just went to the top of my to-do list. Though you'd make things a whole lot easier if you kept your fingers out of my face." He leaned closer.

Her cheeks bloomed a bright pink. "I'm serious."

He schooled his features in an innocent expression. "It's

only a kiss." The one-kiss theory had burned to ashes the moment his lips touched hers. He didn't know exactly what he wanted anymore. Come to think of it, *more* was exactly what he wanted. He leaned forward.

"I'm saying no," she whispered, not sounding all that sure.

That did it. He'd lost the battle. Sure, he could push and enjoy a few more kisses, but he'd lose more than he'd gain. She said no. *End of story.*

Carrie's heart flip-flopped as Aaron took her other foot in his hands. "What are you doing now?" She tried to pull away, but he held on.

"Finishing what I started." He scooped sudsy water over the arch and gave her foot the same careful attention he'd lavished on the one already immersed in water.

"You don't have to do that." She barely recognized her own voice.

"I want to." His eyes were dark and bottomless.

She looked away and pressed her hands to her stomach, hoping to stop the quivering at her core. "Something happened back there, Aaron." She pulled her foot from his slippery hand and plopped it into the pot alongside her other foot.

He rubbed the back of his neck. "A lot happened back there. I should have gone to church with you."

"I'm talking about the angel. Ross saw something. I'm sure of it."

A crooked smile parted his lips. "Maybe so."

Her hands clenched into tight fists. "Don't agree just to shut me up."

He stood. "Do you have any first aid cream?"

"And don't change the subject."

"I want to treat the cuts on your feet," he chided.

"I can take care of my own feet." Barely maintaining control of the seething mix of anger, fear, and confusion that threatened to overwhelm her, Carrie held out a trembling hand. "Give me that towel."

After a long moment, he drew the towel from his shoulder and handed it to her. She patted her sore feet dry and inspected the abrasions and bruises. A raw scratch ran the length of one arch. "There's first aid cream in the bathroom cabinet."

He left the room.

She took deep breaths in an attempt to quiet the aftershocks from the fear she'd experienced in the cemetery and the kisses. *Oh my, the man could kiss.* The fear blended with a nerve tingling longing as she listened to him rummage through her medicine cabinet. Hands fisted in the ripped, stained skirt of her dress, she fought the overwhelming desire to cry.

He stepped back into the room much too soon. He knelt in front of her, and she bit her lip holding back tears. She didn't deserve this attention. His strong hands rubbed salve into her feet, and she'd never in her life felt so cared for.

"Tell me Ross's last name." He drew his thumb along the arch of her foot, tracing a scratch.

The sting of medicine was minor compared to the throbbing sensation racing up her leg straight to her heart. She shook her head, not wanting thoughts of Ross to mar the moment.

"C'mon, Carrie. A guy deserves to know the name of the creep that sneaks up behind him and bashes him over the head."

"What are you talking about?" She cupped his cheek in her palm. Tears ran down her cheeks.

"Aw, sweetheart." The cushion next to her dipped, and his arms folded around her. "Don't cry."

But his request came too late. Carrie let out a loud wail and rubbed her eyes with her fists. Tears dripped off her chin. A soft cloth dabbed at her face. Taking the handkerchief he offered, she blew her nose.

So much had happened. She could have lost Benny. And Aaron, too. She tried to stem the flood of tears but sobs tore at her throat. She leaned into his warm strength and let the tears flow.

Aaron smoothed a hand over Carrie's hair and held her close. Her crying hurt him more than the almost blinding headache he suffered now that the adrenaline rush had subsided. He'd love nothing better than to sit here holding her while he got the complete story out of her. But if he didn't take an aspirin and find a dark room pretty quick, he couldn't guarantee he'd have the strength to leave her side and climb the stairs to his apartment.

Her crying jag tapered off to noisy sniffs and a ragged sigh.

He gave her a squeeze before he stood. He was careful not to move too fast for fear his head would roll off his shoulders.

She sniffed again. "Where are you going?"

"To get ice for your ankle." Cool air wafted across his face when he opened the freezer. He poked through the usual assortment of frozen vegetables, ground beef, and— packages of pantyhose?

He pulled one of the thin cardboard envelopes from the neatly stacked pile and stared at it. A fine mist instantly covered the little cellophane window.

This explanation oughtta be good.

A bag of frozen peas in one hand and package of pantyhose in the other, he returned to the living room. He tossed the envelope in her lap. "Found these in your freezer." He slid the pot of water aside and moved a footstool closer.

Benny began to fuss. She set the pantyhose on the couch cushion and lifted him to her lap. "That's where I keep them."

Settling her foot on the stool, he knelt and tested the ankle with his fingers before draping the bag of peas over it. "Most women keep them in a dresser drawer."

"That's not ice. And how do you know what most women do?"

Startled by her question, he lifted his head too fast and felt a sharp pain. The agony would have brought him to his knees except—he was already there. Closing his eyes, he rubbed a hand across his brow. Thinking straight was becoming more difficult by the minute, and he still needed to secure the apartment before he could stretch out on his couch and succumb to oblivion. "You have one lonely tray of ice. Enough for one, maybe two, glasses of lemonade."

"I don't have room for more trays."

"Because..." He pointed at the bright blue cardboard envelope she'd shoved aside.

She huffed and stuck her chin in the air. "June told me the cold strengthens the nylon fibers."

"Who's June?"

"A woman I work with."

"And who's Ross? I need his last name."

82

A long moment passed where the only one making any noise was Benny. He was winding up for another go at trying to get nourishment.

"I didn't see him hit you on the head."

Her whispered statement sent his mind scrambling to censor the anger eating at him. He'd give her only the basics. "After I dropped you off, I fueled the car before pulling over to vacuum out the sand. With the vacuum running I didn't hear anyone come up behind me. I think it's more than coincidental that you ran into trouble at the same time." He rose and gestured toward Benny. "He's hungry."

"There's a bottle in the fridge. Set it in a pan of hot water to warm."

Between the pain in his head and the ache in his heart, the small task loomed with monumental proportions. *Warming a baby bottle. Who would have thought?* He checked the lock on the kitchen door before returning to the living room with the heated bottle. "Here you go." He handed her the small bottle and backed away. "Don't answer either door." Pain hammered at his temples. "Ross has stepped off the deep end." He glanced at Benny. "Wish you trusted me enough to talk to me about what happened."

Setting the lock on her door, he stepped into the foyer.

"St. Martin. His last name is St. Martin."

Her whispered words managed to penetrate the banging in his head. He checked the lock on the front door and climbed the steps to his apartment. The windows were opened wide and the place was still steamy. He switched on the giant fan. The motor whirred to life. The large paddles gathered speed and sent the pages from the morning paper flying across the room. Taking out his phone, Aaron moved to stand in front of the gale force wind.

Jason answered on the second ring.

"I got the name." He didn't bother with the niceties. "St. Martin. Ross St. Martin."

"I'm on it. You sound bad. What happened?"

Aaron sucked in a deep breath. He hoped he didn't have a concussion. "Let's say, I've had my first run in with the man, and I owe him some hurt."

"You need me out there?"

"Nah. Aspirin will do. Just find me everything you can on him."

"Don't try to be a hero, man."

"Yeah. Later." Ending the call, he reached for the bottle of pain relievers sitting on the kitchen counter and shook out two. He tossed them to the back of his throat and swallowed before stripping off his t-shirt. Stretched out on the couch, he let the wind blow over his heated skin. Drifting off, his last thought was of Carrie, safe in his arms.

Carrie patted Benny's back. He'd finished his bottle and fallen asleep. She wouldn't be far behind him. Stifling a yawn, she poked the bag of peas with her good foot. They were beginning to defrost.

Something fell to the floor. She peaked over the edge of the couch. The package of pantyhose Aaron had pulled from the freezer lay on the carpet. The sharp knife of jealousy jabbed close to her heart. How did he know where "most women" kept their hose?

She sighed. "Don't be stupid, Carrie Anne." The man didn't need to have personal knowledge. He was being his logical self. She touched her lips. His kiss had rocked her deep inside her soul.

Rearranging pillows and balancing the bag of frozen peas

on her ankle, she curled up with Benny and closed her eyes. But the memory of Ross screaming at her to remove Aaron from her life *or he'll be hurt* popped her eyelids open again.

Aaron suspected Ross of hitting him over the head. If that was true, he'd already been hurt because of her. Ross was prepared to hurt him again.

Shivering, Carrie pulled a crocheted afghan from the back of the couch. She nuzzled Benny who was sweetly cocooned in the deep sleep of the innocent. Somehow she had to keep Aaron and Benny safe. But how? She was physically no match for Ross, and she couldn't go to the police. Ross had friends in the police department. He'd made it clear she risked losing Benny if she ran to them for help. She rubbed a gentle hand along the curve of Benny's back. She would never willingly let go of him.

What if her own mother hadn't wanted to let go of Carrie?

Carrie gasped. The possibility sent a tremor through her. A tear trickled sideways over the bridge of her nose and fell to her baby's soft cheek. She pushed the unsettling thoughts aside, refusing to follow the "what ifs."

The lone tear was soon followed by another, and then another. She gave up trying to stop the flow and wept. For Benny. For Aaron. For all her mistakes that had brought the three of them to this point in time.

A chime penetrated the muzzy fog of sleep. Carrie pushed aside the itchy afghan. Half asleep, she fumbled in Benny's diaper bag for her phone. "Ello?"

"Is *he* with you?"

The malice threading through Ross's voice cleared her sleep-befuddled brain in an instant. She struggled to sit up without waking Benny. The mushy bag of peas slid off her ankle, and she kicked it to the floor.

"Well is he?" His sharp voice pierced her ear.

"No." The hope she could reason with him won out over the desire to hang up. "Why are you doing this?"

His humorless laugh raised goose bumps on her arms. "Because we were good together, babe. Or have you forgotten?"

She sucked in her breath. A wave of nausea passed over her. Before she could reply he went on.

"Do you remember the night we met?" A wicked purr vibrated through his words.

"Stop." Her throat constricted with fear.

"Stop? It's too late to use that word with me."

Hot shame poured through Carrie as the memories tumbled one after the other through her mind. The catered dinner had been a political fundraiser. All the town bigwigs were in attendance. With many beautiful women in the room, Ross chose to shower *her* with attention.

When she set the rolls on the table, he'd brushed her hand with his fingertips. As she served dinner, he'd touched her arms. At the end of the meal while removing the dinner plates, she'd stepped close to the table. His warm hand grazed the back of her knee.

Carrie's stomach rolled. She'd lapped up the attention like a starving kitten. *Wanted.* She'd never felt that before. Certainly not as a foster child, constantly moving from one home to another. After the dinner, his invitation had been irresistible.

Pushing aside the memories, she dragged in a shuddering breath. "I shouldn't have gone with you that night. What I did was wrong." The night led to days, followed by—*forgive me, God*—more nights.

"You were wrong to leave me."

For a moment the timid girl she'd once been tried to push words of appeasement from her raw throat, but she managed to swallow them. She rubbed her arm where an old injury sometimes ached. "You were abusive." She'd tolerated a lot in the name of love, or rather, what she'd thought was love. *So naïve.* "I was afraid you'd hurt Benny."

"If you had done as I asked, you wouldn't have a baby. You'd still be with me."

Carrie's heart trembled as she ran her hand over Benny sleeping peacefully beside her. "Ross, please leave us alone. Go live your life. Let us go on with ours."

"Ah. But you chose to have the baby. As the father I have every right to be part of my son's life, don't you think?"

Dear God. She prayed to calm the panic filling her. "You didn't want him!"

"I made a mistake."

Ross admitting he'd been wrong? Carrie's panic morphed into terror as alarm bells clanged in her mind. "What do you want?" Her throat hurt with each word.

"You always were such a simple little thing." His sigh of mock patience hissed across the connection. "There's a growing trend for politicians to admit their mistakes. Come clean, so to speak."

"You don't hold a political office."

"I have time to show the town folk I'm a loving husband and father."

Carrie gasped. "Husband? Who—?"

"You, babe. Marry me."

The sweetness in his voice made her sick to her stomach.

"I'm trying to do the right thing here, Carrie. I can give you and Benny a much better place than that seedy apartment you're living in."

The right thing. For the wrong reason. Her apartment was clean and bright and filled with peace. A peace she'd never have with him. Before Benny was born, she'd longed for a fairytale wedding with Ross. She'd dreamed of a home with him. But the beautiful dream had turned into a nightmare.

"It's too late." She pushed the words past the lump in her throat. Pulling Benny onto her lap, she curled over him protectively. "Leave us alone. Please."

"I'll say this one more time." His voice rang hard. "Get rid of the goon that's trying to protect you, or I'll get rid of him for you. Oh, and check the front step. I left something for you."

The connection went dead.

With growing dread, Carrie rose and piled pillows around Benny. What could Ross have possibly left for her? A tremor ran through her. Ross had been close—on the doorstep—while she'd slept. Whatever he'd left, she needed to dispose of it before Aaron found out.

Hobbling to her apartment door, she unfastened the lock and peeked into the foyer. Nothing was out of place or different in the small entry. Opening her door wider, she slipped out and peered through the narrow window at the side of the front door. A bouquet of pink and white roses wrapped in green florist paper lay on the step. Carrie unlatched the deadbolt. Fearing that Ross was on the other side of the door ready to push his way into her apartment, she gathered her courage before opening the door a crack.

Nothing happened.

A rush of relief helped her move faster on her bum ankle. She grabbed the bouquet and stepped back toward the door.

A strong hand latched onto her arm and yanked her backwards through the door so fast she didn't have time to scream.

Whirling about she stopped, face to face with Aaron.

His cheeks flushed with anger, the muscle in his jaw jumped with agitation. "What are you doing?" He spoke from between clenched teeth.

She clutched the flowers to her like a shield and thrust out her chin. "What does it look like I'm doing?"

His gaze fell to the flowers, and his face became an expressionless mask. "Who are they from?"

Trying to buy time to think, she buried her nose in the soft petals and murmured, "That's none of your business." Aaron had to stop trying to protect her and Benny.

Aaron pressed closer, crowding her against the door. "I'm making this my business." He snatched the small white envelope from among the blossoms and tore it open. His jaw worked as he silently read the card. Slowly he lifted his gaze to her face. His eyes were bleak. "Who is he?"

Taking the ivory card from him, Carrie read it. "We are meant for each other. Always." She scrambled for an explanation. Perhaps this was the break she needed. "Someone I'm seeing." Her heart grew heavy beneath the weight of the lie. Her statement had the desired effect.

He backed off, his face dark and unreadable.

A cry came from her apartment. Benny was awake.

Breathing a silent thank you, Carrie skirted around Aaron and entered her apartment. *This was for the best.* He'd leave her alone and be safe. *If he finds out, will he forgive me? Will God forgive me?* Sick at heart, she closed the door behind her.

Busy street, Margin Street. Burt Campbell gnawed on a granola bar and sipped from his water bottle. The black

SUV had cruised the street for fifteen minutes before disappearing. Ten minutes later the vehicle appeared again and parked a block away. The man delivering flowers had been an uptight dude. He tried to appear nonchalant, but Burt knew scared when he saw it. The man didn't even bother to knock on the woman's door. Dropped the flowers on the step and left. *A real Casanova, that one.*

Pulling a dingy handkerchief from his pocket, Burt wiped it across his brow. The shade of the maple tree he'd parked beneath didn't cut the heat of the day by much and the foul stink of skunk still lingered in the upholstery. The cleaning charge that the car rental company would add to his client's invoice would take a little explaining, but that was okay with Burt. At least today had been interesting. He'd bet a granola bar, his client didn't know about the baby.

A self-appointed observer of human nature, he wondered which man was the daddy, Casanova or the biker. If he had to pick one, he'd have said the biker. But to be sure, he'd watch a bit longer before reporting. Then he'd collect the balance of his fee and find another job. Preferably someplace where you couldn't fry eggs on the dashboard of a car.

Chapter Ten

Aaron took a sip of coffee before wiping his mouth with the back of his hand. A cool ocean breeze played across his arms as he sat sidesaddle on his parked bike.

The scenic overlook followed a curve in the beach road along a strip of rugged coastline. Rocks and giant boulders claimed rights to both the sand and the sea. Off to the right, the dark finger of the rock jetty stretched out into the heaving ocean. Treacherous and inhospitable, the scenery fit his mood.

Another sleepless night—this one spent on his bike. Speeding along Interstate 95 he'd tried to outrun the desolation that threatened to engulf him. When that didn't work he'd headed back to town, hoping to find a little entertainment to take his mind off a feisty redhead and her miniature sidekick.

He took another swallow of lukewarm coffee. In this town, Sunday night had been quieter than a church on Monday morning. *Sheesh!* His big excitement had come down to cruising the streets and dodging road kill.

And now, here he was on one of those quiet Monday

mornings watching the sun rise from the ocean's dark horizon painting the world peach and pink. A beautiful beginning to another stinking, rotten day.

Aaron scratched his bristly jaw.

A gull poked about in the rocks below.

When had he become so thick headed? Carrie didn't want him around, but he'd kept pushing.

Tossing back the last of his coffee, he crushed the foam cup in his fist. He cast an angry glare in the general direction of up. Stupidly, he'd begun to think God had a plan for him. That maybe, for the first time ever, he was in the right place at the right time. Carrie Lillibridge needed help. He had the expertise to help her. He'd just begun to unravel the mess then *BAM*. Out of nowhere, here came lover boy with flowers.

He gazed balefully at the sky. "Why? Why bring me on the scene just so a woman can knock me on my keester?" Irritated, he walked to a strategically placed public trash bin and tossed his crumpled coffee cup. "Point taken. You don't have to worry about me making any more of a jerk out of myself than I already have."

The sun gilded the wet rocks and warmed the early morning air. He rubbed the back of his neck and probed the sore lump on his head. His gut told him his attacker had been Carrie's ex-boyfriend. Aaron would take great pleasure extracting his pound of flesh in revenge. Carrie would most likely work up a fine head of steam trying to protect the worthless yahoo.

He pulled his keys from his pocket. A neon yellow ponytail holder was tangled in them. Chest burning, he stared at the stretchy fabric before pulling it free. He hooked it over a finger and drew it back, aiming at the unsuspecting seagull. At the last minute he folded. The dumb bird was only looking for breakfast. He should do the same before meeting Mr. Beedle at the church.

Fingering the ponytail holder, he jammed it back in his pocket. No way could he go home with Carrie there. He didn't trust himself. Sleep deprived as he was, he'd either chew her out or kiss her. Neither action struck him as a good option. He mounted the Harley. The heavy rumble of the engine vibrated through his restless body. He hungered for something other than ham and eggs, but they'd have to do.

Seated at her desk, the church secretary stared at Aaron. Behind the thick lens of her glasses, her eyes were the size of shooter marbles, and her lips were puckered into a perfect "O."

He looked bad—probably like he'd spent the night on his bike. But you'd think in her position, the woman would have enough sense to at least *try* and hide her reaction. He leaned over her desk. "I said, is Mr. Beedle here?"

The little old blue-hair nodded but other than that didn't move a muscle. He had the urge to slap his hand on her desk just to see how high she'd jump.

The custodian's entrance into the office saved her.

"Here to see me?" Mr. Beedle pinned him with a hard glare.

Aaron braced his legs apart and crossed his arms over his chest. At the last minute he neutralized his hard cop scowl. *Idiot! Terrorizing the elderly.* He dropped his arms to his sides. "I'm here to help repair the window." Belatedly he added, "Sir."

Mr. Beedle stared at him for a long moment. "Follow me." He led Aaron to the basement of the church. In a spacious room tucked away behind a plain brown door there resided an impressive array of tools and equipment. "Hold this." He handed Aaron a cylinder of window glazing and a small putty knife. From high on a shelf he took a cardboard packet wrapped in tape.

Aaron frowned at the pile of cardboard on the shelf. "You have panes of glass on hand?"

Mr. Beedle led the way out of the room and closed the door. "Yep."

"So I'm not the first person to break one?"

The old man shrugged a khaki clad shoulder. "It happens." With slow steps he ascended the stairs. His voice rang hollow in the enclosed stairwell. "Is she all right?"

With sludge for a brain, Aaron needed a moment to follow the custodian's train of thought. A nanosecond later the torment returned. "Yeah. Last I saw her, anyway."

The old man stopped at the top of the stairs. "When you *last* saw *her*?"

"That's what I said." Aaron fought to hold onto his patience. Mr. Beedle was asking because he cared.

"What time was that?"

"Late yesterday afternoon." Unease crawled along Aaron's spine.

Mr. Beedle continued his slow shuffle down the hall to the door in need of repair. Using the claw of his hammer, he removed the nails from the board tacked over the empty pane. "What happened?"

The old man wasn't quitting with the questions. Aaron opened the glazing and picked up the corrugated cardboard packet that held a single pane of glass. He peeled off the tape holding the layers together. "She doesn't need me." He swallowed his pride. "She's got some other guy to defend her." Not for the life of him would he admit Carrie wanted him to leave her alone.

Mr. Beedle stopped prying at the nails and frowned. "So where was this *other guy* yesterday when she needed him?"

"I have no idea." Aaron pulled the last little bit of tape away from the cardboard. "Probably out buying the flowers he left on the doorstep."

"The doorstep?" Mr. Beedle shook his head. "What man worth his salt does that?"

Aaron grimaced. "I wouldn't know." He gingerly held the loose sandwich of corrugate and glass.

Mr. Beedle turned to the window, muttering to himself. "A man buys a lady flowers, he wants to reap the rewards. At least a hug. If he's lucky, a kiss. Leave them on the step? Don't seem right to me."

The old man had a point. The kisses were definitely worth collecting. The back of Aaron's neck prickled. "Maybe he thought leaving them for her to find was romantic."

The old man's snort echoed in the hallway. "Fool. If I ever meet him, I'll tell him what—"

The shock of realization jolted through Aaron causing him to fumble the packet.

The sharp shatter of glass silenced Mr. Beedle's tirade. He stared at the floor. "Trustees are gonna have to increase my budget."

Still holding the cardboard, Aaron studied the glittering shards on the floor and toes of his boots. "I've lived above her about a week. I've chased a prowler. Fought an ex-boyfriend. Got hit over the head—"

"When?"

"Yesterday morning. Before I broke your window."

"Trouble's following you, young man."

Aaron stared at Mr. Beedle. "Didn't have any trouble like this before—" *Carrie.* The common denominator in every

95

incident was Carrie. Trouble was following *her*. Not some romantic fool courting her with flowers.

Glass crunched underfoot. "She's at work. I want to check on her. I don't know if Benny is with her or at Thelma's." He opened the door and slipped outside.

Mr. Beedle stared at him through the empty windowpane.

Aaron ran for his bike calling over his shoulder, "Sorry about the glass. I'll pay for it." He fought the panic rising in him. "Okay, God. Maybe I haven't finished making a fool of myself."

Holding the desk phone's receiver to her ear, Carrie punched in the next number. A mechanical click and a recorded message followed the ringing on the other end of the line.

Another answering machine.

"This is Carrie at the Neighborhood Center with a reminder that Food Co-op is this Saturday morning at nine o'clock. See you there." She hung up and sighed. Only twenty more calls before she finished.

The distinct rumble of a motorcycle caused her heart to skip a beat as she dialed Mrs. Luzzi. Keeping the receiver glued at her ear, Carrie stood and leaned across her desk. Favoring her aching ankle, she poked her head through the sliding window separating her desk from the hallway. Tiny, white-haired June stood on a stepstool posting flyers on the bulletin board inside the glass entrance door.

Through the phone line she heard a quavering, "Hello?"

"Hello, Mrs. Luzzi. This is Carrie at the Neighborhood Center." The poor dear was hard of hearing. Stretched across her desk, Carrie found it next to impossible to inhale as much air as she needed to yell.

"Who?"

The silhouette of a man materialized outside the door.

"This is Carrie at the Neighborhood Center."

"Oh, hello Carrie."

The door swung open.

"I'm calling to remind you Food Co-op is this Saturday." Carrie's heart leapt as Aaron charged indoors, stripping off his sunglasses as he came.

Mrs. Luzzi's voice oscillated loud then soft. "What did you say?"

"Food Co-op is—" Carrie gasped. In his haste, Aaron walked straight into June.

"Yes? What about Food Co-op?"

Mrs. Luzzi's question barely registered as Carrie watched June sway and tumble off the stepstool into Aaron's arms.

"Hello? Carrie? Are you there? Hello? Hello?"

"Y-Yes, Mrs. Luzzi, I'm here. Um…." Carrie couldn't take her gaze off Aaron. He appeared at a loss with what to do with June, the past her prime *femme fatale* reclining in his arms. For whatever the stupid reason, the sight irked Carrie.

"Carrie, is Food Co-op this Saturday?"

"Yes." Carrie's shout drew Aaron's attention. The impact of his intense gaze made her duck back from the window. "See you at nine, Mrs. Luzzi. Goodbye."

Aaron came to her window holding June.

His gaze swept over Carrie, triggering a swooshing in her belly—like autumn leaves flying in the wind. "I see you've met June."

"Who?"

"June." Carrie nodded her head toward the tittering senior citizen he held.

"Oh. Yeah." With care he set June on her feet. "The frozen stockings lady. Nice to meet you, ma'am." He offered his hand, and June grasped it, giggling like a schoolgirl.

Annoyed by the two of them, Carrie said the first thing that popped into her head. "Pantyhose. If they were stockings I'd have to wear a garter belt."

Aaron swung around, his eyes riveted on her. His warm gaze sent heat flaming across her cheeks.

Shut your mouth, Carrie Anne. "Don't even *think* of going there, Aaron." Carrie huffed and plopped into her office chair. Thankful it had casters, she tucked as much of herself as she could fit beneath the desk. Before she could tell the arrogant beast to stop staring at her like *that* he caught sight of the flowers. The warm interest on his face slipped away.

Carrie's heart sank to the depths of her tummy. With June as an enthusiastic observer, she went on the offensive, grasping the edge of her desk. "What are you doing here?"

He pulled his gaze away from the offending blossoms. "I wanted to check that you got to work okay." He lifted his chin toward the flowers. "Lover boy's never around when you need him."

June squeaked. Her eyes were round as pennies.

Desperate to keep June from saying anything that would give away yesterday's lie, Carrie sent her friend a pleading look before addressing Aaron. "You don't know that." She pulled a pout meant to put him off. "You know nothing about him."

He raised one eyebrow and leaned his elbows on the window ledge. His shoulders filled the open side of the window. "Enlighten me."

Dwarfed by his presence, she refused to give an inch of ground by rolling her chair back. She tucked a wayward strand of hair into her ponytail. "My love life is none of your concern."

Through the closed half of the window she saw June clap a hand over her mouth, muffling a chirp of surprise.

He shifted his stance, backing off a bit. "Show me the daycare."

"You're scared to death of infants and toddlers," she said.

He scowled. "I want to check on Benny."

Happy to thwart his high-handed tactics, Carrie smiled sweetly. "He's not here."

He lunged toward the window alarming Carrie into scooting her chair backwards, almost tipping over in her haste.

"Where is he?"

"Don't yell at me. And June, quit your squeaking!" Carrie stood. She'd reached her limit. "What is wrong with you, Aaron? Why are you checking on me?" His tight expression and low controlled voice sent a shiver of apprehension down her spine.

"Because no matter how I look at the events of the past few days, you and your baby are in trouble up to your ponytail. You know it but are too stubborn to ask for help." His breath bellowed in and out of his lungs as though he'd run hard and fast. "A stalker is not to be ignored. Even when you know the person stalking you and think you can handle him. Ross will become bolder and more dangerous."

June gasped, her gaze flying between Carrie and Aaron.

Carrie licked her dry lips. "What makes you so sure of that?"

"Experience."

She crossed her arms, ready to pursue what exactly that meant.

June took advantage of the momentary silence. "Thelma's." She glanced apologetically at Carrie but kept talking. "Benny is at Thelma's today."

Carrie groaned in frustration.

Aaron stared at the tiny woman. It was all the encouragement she needed to continue. "I told her to report that awful man to the police."

He pointed at Carrie. "You. Stay here."

She sputtered before finding the words to speak. "Don't point your finger at me, Aaron Black!"

Running toward the door he paid no attention to her.

She yanked her purse from the drawer and fumbled through it for her car keys. Hurrying as fast as her ankle allowed, she left the tiny office.

In the hallway, June touched her arm. "He said to stay here."

"I don't take orders from him. I'm taking an early lunch. Cover for me." The hurt expression on the elderly woman's face cut through Carrie's heart. When had she become so callous? "Please? If Benny's in danger—"

"Go. But I wish you'd listen to your young man."

Hurrying down the hall listening to the growl of Aaron's motorcycle tearing out of the parking lot, Carrie called over her shoulder, "He's not mine."

"Then can I have him?" June asked.

Carrie opened the door. She *so* did not hear that correctly, but she still answered, *"No."* Just in case.

Chapter Eleven

Aaron sped around the corner onto Margin Street. His wraparound sunglasses cut the glare of the sun as he scanned the street. A sedan sat in the deep shade of a large maple tree. There was no sign of St. Martin's vehicle. He should've felt better, but the knot in his gut wouldn't go away.

Feet on the ground on either side of the bike, he walked it to a stop behind Thelma's car and cut the engine. At the familiar roar of an old car pushed to its limit, he swung around. He should have known Carrie would follow him.

Sprinting up Thelma's front steps, he rapped on the purple door.

"Is everything okay?" Carrie limped across the lawn.

"You should have stayed at the Center where I knew you were safe." He knocked on the door, harder this time.

Carrie climbed the steps and stood beside him. Her hair hung in wispy feathers around her face. Soon her ponytail holder would land on the floorboards of the porch. When it did he'd scoop it up.

She frowned and pushed the doorbell, calling out, "Auntie?"

They didn't hear an answering shout or *pat-pat* of footsteps coming to the door.

"I'll check around back." The hair on Aaron's neck prickled. He scanned the street before ducking behind the house. Inside the doorbell pealed again. Carrie had stayed on the porch. He knocked on the kitchen door and tried the handle. Locked.

Through the lacy curtain he didn't see anything out of the ordinary in the kitchen. From where he stood on the top step, the yard was in order. He scrubbed a hand across his face in frustration as he circled the house, coming back to the front porch. Taking the steps two at a time, he paused long enough to grab the hot pink ponytail holder that lay on the top step. He slid it into his jeans pocket.

Carrie's hands and face were pressed against the window of the front door. "I can't see anything." She glanced at him, anxiety lining her face. "Her car is here. Where are they?"

"The back bedroom window is open a couple of inches. I'm gonna pop the screen and climb in."

Carrie's vivid green eyes grew wide. "That's breaking and entering."

"No?" Mock disbelief laced his voice.

"Be serious. What if we're arrested?"

The feeling that something was wrong put a lid on his teasing. "That would happen only if Thelma pressed charges which we know wouldn't happen." He grasped her elbow and steered her toward the steps. "Com'on. You can hold the chair for me."

She dragged her feet.

"Our other option is to call the police."

"No!" Instantly she increased her pace.

Placing a wire mesh chair from the patio beneath the

window, he showed her where he wanted her to stand to hold it steady.

"This is the room Benny sleeps in when he's here. Can you see him?" She worried her bottom lip with her teeth.

"Nope. Just hold onto the chair."

The old screen fit loosely in the frame. Shaking his head over the poor security, he inserted the blade of his jackknife between the screen and the casing. He slid the blade down until he hit resistance. Using pressure, he sprang the latch. He repeated the process on the opposite side and then pried the bottom of the screen away from the sill. Wiggling the screen up and down, he unhooked the top.

"Here you go." He passed it to Carrie.

"How'd you know how to do that?" She glared at him suspiciously.

"It's a guy thing." He pushed on the window. It didn't budge. He shoved harder.

Carrie sniffed. "Hurry up."

He banged a fist along each side of the wood frame hoping the window hadn't been painted shut. Putting all his muscle into it, he tried to raise the sash. It gave a little.

"Aaron." Her voice a loud whisper, Carrie tugged his pant leg. "I think I hear someone."

He paused, heard the slam of a car door out on the street and muted voices. "Probably a neighbor."

"Maybe it's Thelma. I'll check."

"We should be so lucky. Give me another minute here." Using the side of his fist, he rapped the frame again. Bracing himself, he gave a mighty upward push on the window. It took several more times of banging and pushing before the wood groaned and let go. The sash banged into the stops, rattling the windowpanes. The chair Aaron stood on rocked. Unable to catch his balance, the chair tipped onto two legs.

He threw himself across the sill afraid if he went down, he'd fall on top of Carrie. Draped half in and half out of the window, he heard the chair fall to its side. His feet dangled in midair.

"Carrie?"

There was no reply.

Muttering, he kicked with his legs and thrust himself into the room. He landed face first in a laundry basket filled with clean, sweet smelling baby clothes. He tucked and rolled onto his back. Two elderly women and a beaming Carrie stared down at him.

"The car I heard *was* Thelma coming home." Carrie cuddled Benny close.

Her happy expression caused his heart to hammer. "You were supposed to hold the chair." He rose on his elbows. Scattered across his chest and on the floor were small t-shirts and other bits of unidentifiable baby clothing. He pulled a soft piece of cloth from his shoulder and pitched it toward the basket.

As if one, Thelma and the other woman rushed him with hands outstretched to rescue the rest of the clothing.

He stood and Thelma snatched at the clothes falling off his chest. "Pauline took us out to lunch." She nodded at her friend who was busy folding a blanket with a picture of a teddy bear on it. "I'm sorry if we caused you concern."

Out of his element and confused because his instincts had never been so wrong, Aaron tugged at the ties of a tiny bib wrapped around his arm and handed it to Thelma. "Let me know the next time." He bolted for the front door.

Unable to shake the tension eating at him, Aaron walked to the back of the house and returned the chair to the patio. His phone rang. "Black."

"Some situation you got yourself into there, man."

"Hey, Jase." Relief washed through Aaron. He sat in the chair. "What do you have?"

"Ross St. Martin, son of heavy-weight Jonas St. Martin. Big fish in a little pond. Surprised you haven't run across his name in the newspaper."

Aaron rubbed his forehead, remembering the Sunday paper scattered across his living room. He'd never gotten around to reading it.

"The family has a finger in almost every pie, no matter what the flavor." Aaron's terse response drew a chuckle for his friend. "So you ready to call in the cavalry?"

"Not yet." He reviewed the last few hours for Jason's benefit. "I'm losing my touch."

Jason whistled. "Your gut saved my skin more times than I care to remember."

"They were out having an early lunch." He swatted at a mosquito buzzing him. "I had them kidnapped and in a car trunk."

"We're trained to expect the worst."

"Yeah, well, I looked like a fool this time." Aaron rubbed the back of his neck.

"So you're good now that they're home?"

Was he? A sense of foreboding haunted him. Aaron slapped his palm on the arm of the chair. "No."

"Then figure out what's bothering you."

His friend's confidence felt misplaced. Aaron blurted, "You still pray?"

"What?"

"You know, talk to God. Do you?"

Jason let the question hang between them for a moment before he answered. "Yeah. Why?"

"Think He listens?"

"Thought you decided God didn't exist?"

Aaron stood and paced to the edge of the driveway and back. "Carrie's like you. She believes."

"I'll keep you both in my prayers. You might want to try saying a few yourself."

"We'll see." No way was he willing to admit he'd already prayed a few times. Not even to Jason. Their conversation had begun to sound—girlie. "Later." He cut the connection and sat listening to the neighborhood activity and the three women inside the house. Carrie's happy giggle captured his attention. He groaned. His insides were in a stew over the spirited redhead. He stretched, hoping to ease the tight muscles across his shoulders. It was time to read yesterday's newspaper.

Chapter Twelve

Aaron sat in his kitchen with all the lights off. Twilight cast murky shadows over the street. For the past three days, he'd been vigilantly watching over Thelma, Carrie, and Benny. From the get-go, Carrie had made her feelings clear. She wanted to be left alone. He'd expected that. But this afternoon, even sweet had Thelma lost her patience with him. He'd insisted on taking her grocery shopping. She got downright snippy with him. Her happy disposition evaporated in the face of a threat to her independence.

A sudden flash of light shone in the interior of the gray sedan beneath the maple tree.

Adam bolted upright.

The SUV hadn't been around recently. Had St. Martin hired someone to do his dirty work for him? He'd know soon enough. This morning he'd given Jason the car's license plate number. It had appeared and disappeared at various times over the course of the last few days. No one ever got in or out.

Aaron rubbed a dribble of sweat from his temple. He still hadn't seen the flower guy. If Carrie *was* seeing someone, they weren't crazy in love. He refused to examine the reason this thought brought a measure of satisfaction.

The squeak of Carrie's rocker and her soft voice singing Benny to sleep swirled up through the floorboards and in through the open windows.

Aaron had begun looking forward to her evening routine of rocking and singing Benny to sleep. He knew she was safely in for the night. He'd get up a few times, scout around the house and Thelma's place, but that would be the extent of his nighttime activities.

The sedan's engine turned over and the headlights blinked on. The car pulled away from the sidewalk and traveled down the street to the corner where it turned out of view.

Time to hit the rack. Aaron put his boots next to the door before going into the bedroom where he stretched out on top of the bed. The heat was oppressive. He'd rest a minute then bring the fan in from the living room.

An explosion ripped his eardrums. The shock wave threw him to the floor. Sifting through the sawdust, he tried to find the baby. The flames licked hot at his back as panic squeezed his chest. The baby was crying.

Aaron woke clutching the bedding. His heart banged painfully against his ribs. *The dream. Again.* He groaned and rubbed his ears, the baby's cries still ringing in them. He swung his feet off the side of the bed and paused.

A soft voice mingled with the cries. The murmured words were not in his head. They were real and coming from the apartment below. *Carrie and Benny.*

He checked his watch. One o'clock in the morning. Time to haul on his boots and do his neighborhood check.

Glad to leave the stuffy apartment and the haunting dream behind, Aaron carried his boots down the stairs to the front porch where he sat on the step to pull them on. The cool night air sliced through the lingering brain fog clearing his head.

Happy that the sedan hadn't returned to the spot beneath the tree, he walked the perimeter of Carrie's yard. Golden light and Benny's cries spilled from her open kitchen window.

He crossed into Thelma's yard. Finding nothing out of the ordinary, he slipped through the high hedge that bordered both backyards and stood in the deep shadow, listening and studying the neighborhood that was now familiar to him.

Satisfied that all was well, he ducked through the hedge and worked his way to the front porch where he settled in Carrie's wicker chair. Between the dream and Benny's crying he was wide-awake. Hopefully the baby settled down so Carrie could go to bed.

Aaron stared at his watch. How did a screaming baby actually make time stand still? He'd sat here for twenty minutes. The baby had cried himself out several times. But the lull didn't last more than a few minutes before he'd start again with renewed vigor. How Carrie hung onto her patience was a mystery to him, but her soft crooning voice never wavered.

His experience with babies amounted to zip, but from what he'd seen of Benny, the child was pretty mellow, making this crying jag unusual. Was he sick? Aaron shifted in his chair. What if Benny had a fever? Was Carrie giving Benny enough fluids?

Aaron stood and paced the length of the porch. Maybe Benny needed to go to the hospital. Carrie knew she could ask him to take them, right? He sat and then bounced up to walk the length of the porch again. He paused at the front door. He was dithering like an old man. Checking that the front door locked behind him, he crossed the foyer and rapped on her apartment door. "Carrie?"

Benny's wailing continued, but the soft singing stopped.

"Carrie, it's me. Aaron. What's wrong with Benny?" Would she ignore him? Now that he'd opened his mouth he felt foolish. What did he know about babies?

She answered the door. "I'm sorry he woke you."

"That's okay. Is he sick?"

Exhausted, she stood before him holding the squalling infant. A mélange of baby by-products spotted her t-shirt.

She stood back, and he entered her apartment. Taking her elbow, he guided her into the kitchen. "Does he have a fever?" He spoke loudly to be heard above the baby's racket.

"A small one. His teeth are bothering him." She pushed a ring of squishy plastic beads into his mouth. "This is cold and should soothe his gums."

Benny spit the ring out. A pink stream of liquid followed, spraying the front of Carrie's shirt.

Alarm zinged through Aaron's chest as he fumbled for his keys. "That's blood. I'm taking you both to the hospital. Grab whatever you need. Let's go."

"No, he's okay." She dabbed at Benny's chin with a cloth. "The pain reliever I gave him five minutes ago is a red liquid." She glanced at the motorcycle keys in his hand and gave a tired giggle. "Were you planning on loading us on your bike?"

Anxiety sizzling along every nerve, Aaron jingled the keys in his hand. "Guess that wouldn't work." He shoved them back in his pocket. "You're sure that's the medicine? He didn't bust a vein from screaming?"

She shook her head. "No. He's tougher than that. Here."

Before he could respond, he was holding the baby. He stiffened. "Ah, Carrie? This isn't a good idea." But she'd already stepped out of the room.

Terrified he'd drop Benny if he so much as moved a muscle, Aaron stood frozen in place, gazing into big brown baby eyes. Barely daring to breathe he looked—*really looked*—at Benny. Spiky wet eyelashes, runny nose, and pink bow lips stretched wide in a slobbery gummy grin. He had the sensation of his innards melting like warm chocolate.

"What'd you do?" Carrie stood beside him. "How did you make him stop crying?"

Aaron shook his head, unable to form words around the emotion wedged in his throat.

"Come sit down." Her hand pushed at the center of his back as she urged him forward.

Shuffling like a ninety year old, he walked to the couch without mishap. The broken spring poked his thigh, but he didn't dare shift his weight.

Carrie pressed his arms and the baby into his lap.

She left him no choice but to cradle Benny against his stomach. Looking at her, he blinked, and blinked again. She wore a neon pink sweatshirt and lime green sweatpants. "Have mercy, Carrie." *Was that his voice so hoarse and breathless?*

"What?"

He cleared his throat. "It's two in the morning. Your clothes are blinding me."

"They're clean." She yawned and skimmed a hand across the wrinkles on the front of her shirt. "I'm too tired to go all matchy matchy."

She said something else but he didn't hear it. His brain was spinning like a tiny wheel powered by hamsters on caffeine. Desires he thought he'd squelched into nonexistence years ago, spun into focus. Happy recollections and forgotten dreams tumbled past his mind's eye. *Oh yeah. He was in a heap of trouble.* The danger to him was cataclysmic. If God was listening, he was ready to pray for real, and maybe even listen for an answer.

Carrie leaned forward and wiped the corner of Benny's mouth. "How'd you do it?"

"What?" Aaron's expression was blank.

"Quiet him down?"

He didn't answer. He just stared at the baby in his arms.

Not above using the moment to her advantage, Carrie curled a leg beneath her and rested her cheek against cushiony back of the couch. "Do you have a slew of brothers and sisters?" She was determined, one way or another, to figure out this man.

"No. I'm the only one." With one finger, he pushed a fold of the blanket away from Benny's chin. "I lived with my grandmother."

"Was she nice?"

"The best, though sometimes I didn't think so." A half smile curled the corners of his lips.

Carrie dragged the FLORIDA pillow onto her lap. "Why not?"

"She made me do my chores, finish my homework, and go to church. None of those things fit my idea of cool."

Benny's eyelids drooped. Perhaps he'd kept some of the medicine down.

"At least you had her." The full force of his gaze shifted to her. *Great,* now *you decide to come back from whatever planet you were on.*

"You didn't?"

She shook her head. "No. I grew up in foster care."

"Do you know who your parents are? Where they are?"

She fiddled with the fringe on the pillow. "My mother gave me up as a baby. By the time I was old enough to ask questions, I'd passed through so many different homes no one knew the answers."

"The foster families could have found out from the state agency."

She *tsked*. "I suppose. If they'd cared enough."

He frowned. "You could try to do it yourself now if you want to know."

"Won't change anything." Carrie yawned. "My mother gave me up. She didn't take care of me. I'll never do that to Benny. He'll grow up knowing his mama loves him." She closed her eyes. "Do you want to put him to bed?"

Aaron carefully shifted his weight off the broken spring. "No, I'd hate to wake him. The quiet is nice."

Carrie secured Benny's position by tucking the pillow beneath Aaron's arm. "If your arm falls asleep put him in his crib."

Chapter Thirteen

Carrie opened her eyes and looked into the deep warmth of Aaron's gaze. His muscled bicep rested beneath her cheek. Muddled with sleep, her brain refused to telegraph anything but basic commands. *Get up.* She tried, but the leg she'd tucked beneath her had fallen asleep.

"Be still. You're floundering like a fish on a hook." Aaron's soft voice penetrated her befuddled brain. His eyes were heavy from lack of sleep. The beginnings of a beard darkened his jaw. His smile softened the lines of his face, causing Carrie's tummy to tremble.

Self-conscious, she ran a hand over her hair hoping it wasn't sticking out in too many directions. A glimmer of daylight peeked around the edges of the closed drapes. "What time is it?"

"'Bout six."

It wasn't fair he looked so good. She finger combed her hair. A damp spot darkened his sleeve where she'd drooled in her sleep. *Charming.*

Benny, safely ensconced in Aaron's arms, stretched and blinked.

"You could've placed him in his crib."

Aaron smiled, first at her and then at the baby. With the tip of his finger he traced the shell of one tiny ear. "He's amazing, isn't he?"

Tiny shock waves traveled along Carrie's spine. Aaron was different. The lines of his face were softer. He seemed... at peace.

Benny curled a hand around Aaron's finger, pulled it to his mouth and clamped down.

Aaron chuckled. "Guess he's hungry." The baby and man stared into each other's eyes.

"He's teething." Off kilter, she could barely hear her voice over the pounding of her heart. "Biting on your finger helps his gums feel better." Her heart flip-flopped over the look of delight Aaron flashed her way.

He was scaring her. *She was scaring herself.* Her plan did not include falling in love with this man.

A still small voice wormed its way into her bewildered thoughts. *Maybe this man is part of God's plan for you.*

She jumped up and stumbled on her tingling leg and foot. *Lord, make him go away.* The part of her brain that wasn't paying attention commandeered her mouth. "Stay and I'll make coffee."

"Sounds good."

He was at ease holding Benny when he should be scared to death. She wanted him unnerved, like her. "I'll heat a bottle. You can feed him." *Take that!*

"Okay."

Nooooo. You're supposed to panic and run for the door. Sometime during the night an alien had taken over Aaron's body.

Carrie limped to the doorway of the kitchen and paused

to look at the two males occupying her couch. The big one didn't even notice she was lame. *Hmmph!*

Banging around in the kitchen, she took her pique out on the coffee pot, the mugs, and the spoons.

Four hours ago, Aaron had been afraid to hold Benny. She hadn't understood but accepted his fear. This morning, the goofy expression on his face was akin to love. In her experience, people—more specifically, men—didn't change overnight.

Testing the baby's formula for warmth, she wheeled around and crashed into her nemesis.

He was carrying Benny.

"Here." She shoved the bottle at him. Her heart fluttered when he accepted it with a smile.

"Hey, buddy. Ready for breakfast?"

The gentle timbre in Aaron's voice enthralled her.

He sat at her table, cradling the infant in his arms. His hand engulfed the bottle.

"Like this." She tilted the bottle. "Don't let him suck air."

"Thanks."

Aaron's grin turned Carrie's legs to rubber. Setting two mugs of coffee on the table, she sank into the chair beside him. "You're different this morning."

"Hmm?" Aaron sat mesmerized by the baby intent on draining his bottle.

"Aaron." She leaned closer. "You're feeding Benny. Am I the only one finding this strange?"

He blew out a deep breath. "No. I'm out of my league here."

"Could've fooled me."

His smile flashed devastatingly beautiful. "Guess it's like the Bible says, sometimes God can give us a peace that is beyond all understanding."

Carrie edged closer. "That's the first sensible thing you've said because I'm not understanding any of this, so start talking."

"I…I just…." He struggled for words.

"You're getting red around the gills."

"It's hard to explain."

"Try me."

His thumb stroked back and forth over Benny's onesie clad leg. "Sitting on the couch last night, holding Benny," he shrugged, "I got to thinking."

He paused for so long she prompted him to go on. "About what?"

After a few minutes passed he lifted his gaze from Benny's face to hers. "Let's just say I got a lot off my chest." He shrugged. "I unloaded on God."

"You prayed?"

His gaze shifted back to Benny. "Yeah." Whispering, he added, "For a long time."

A sharp pang pierced Carrie's heart. She knew first hand the changes God could bring about in a person. Aaron was finding his way back to God after a long absence. Would he feel differently about *her* now?

Benny spit the nipple out.

Trying to hide the trembling of her hand, Carrie took the bottle from Aaron. "This change in you is another miracle." She waited for him to argue. Hoped he scoffed at the idea like he had in the past.

Instead, his eyes darkened with warmth, and he tugged on a strand of her hair. "Com'ere." He wound her hair around his finger and drew her mouth closer to his lips.

Oh glory! He was going to kiss her. Her knees shook. Sweet agonizing terror welled as the defensive walls surrounding her heart crumbled, leaving her vulnerable.

"You know," he whispered, "you may be right about that." He planted a soft kiss on her lips.

The touch of his warm mouth stopped her breath in her throat. A rush of longing tumbled through her. In need of air, she leaned back and stared at him. He'd agreed with her. She felt effervescent, as though a carbonated beverage bubbled through her veins.

She took Benny from him. "His diaper needs changing." She bolted from the room.

Carrie peeked into the Community Room. The Friday morning geriatric crowd was line dancing their way to fitness. Smack dab in the middle of the gray hair, floral blouses, and stooped shoulders, Aaron sidestepped with the best of them.

Humming along to the music, Carrie glanced at the black button-down shirt and charcoal tweed sports jacket hanging from a coat hook. This morning, the moment the Center had opened its doors, she and Aaron had searched the Clothes Closet for an outfit for him to wear to church. His change of heart seemed too good to be true. But the clothes on the hook were proof something momentous took place through the night and early this morning while he sat on her couch holding Benny.

His change of attitude about God made him more dangerous to her plans. She wouldn't date a man who didn't believe in God. Now that hurdle was gone. Afraid to examine the happiness bubbling through her, Carrie focused on the exercise class.

After months of participation, Mimi Long continued to step right when she should go left. Aaron did his best to dodge her generous proportions on the side steps. He watched over his shoulder on the back steps to miss stepping on the two tiny women Carrie labeled "*La Petites*." Her friend, June, and Ethel danced close on his heels, giggling like smitten teenyboppers.

His presence energized the entire group. They moved to the Big Band swing music with gusto. What they lacked in synchronization, they made up for with enthusiasm.

The music stopped for a brief break. Those who didn't have to sit to catch their breath crowded around the punch bowl in the corner.

Aaron caught Carrie staring at him. His warm smile rooted her feet to the floor.

He threaded his way through the crowd, his eyes never leaving hers. "This crowd can move." His eyes actually twinkled.

She burst out laughing. "This is top speed for most of them. You've inspired them, and they're out to impress you."

A frown crinkled his brow. "Me?"

Carried leaned toward him and whispered, "June and Ethel are especially enjoying the view."

His frown deepened. "What view? They can't see around me. They aren't any taller than my back pocket."

Carrie nodded sagely. "Exactly."

Understanding spread across his features along with the flush of embarrassment. His lips tipped into a foolish grin, and they both burst out laughing.

He held out his hand. "Come join us." His fingertips brushed over the tender skin of her wrist. "Let's have some fun."

With an air of false bravado, she peeled a ponytail holder off her wrist, and drew her hair back. "All right. But be forewarned, I have a pretty mean side-step." Throwing caution aside, Carrie kicked off her heels and let Aaron pull her to the center of the room.

The first blaring notes of a trumpet filled the room. She hadn't felt this light-hearted in ages. She caught the rhythm and stepped in lively unison with the group. Aaron danced at her side. Rocking steps were followed by a series of quick steps interspersed with quarter turns. One more swivel and her hair flew about her face. Trying not to loose her place, she looked down hoping to catch sight of her ponytail holder, but the bit of stretchy fabric had disappeared under the shuffling feet.

She glanced at Aaron.

He smiled and winked before turning away in another series of turns.

Forgetting about her hair, Carrie concentrated on keeping up with the old folks.

Aaron sat in the wicker chair on the front porch, fiddling with the loop of satiny green fabric he'd snatched off the dance floor earlier today. He'd gotten to it before it was trampled beneath two-dozen pairs of orthopedic shoes.

The gray sedan sat silently on the street, this time under a different tree.

For the hundredth time, he checked his phone, assuring himself he hadn't missed a call from Jason. Behind him the door opened.

Carrie stepped onto the porch. "We're ready to go."

He took the diaper bag and stroller from her. "You need all this to go to the mall?"

"Babies don't travel light." Carrie buckled Benny into his

car seat while Aaron stowed the stroller and diaper bag in the rear of the station wagon.

"You don't have to babysit me. I can go on my own." Carrie got into the front passenger seat and buckled up.

"We've been over this. I know you're perfectly capable of going alone." He backed out of the driveway. "You were shopping long before I arrived on the scene. But I feel better accompanying you. Humor me, okay?"

She sighed and leaned her head against the rest.

In the comfortable silence that fell between them, Aaron's thoughts drifted back to the early morning hours and what had taken place in the quiet of her apartment. With her warmth pressed against his side and the weight of Benny on his lap, he'd struggled with his decision to live a solitary existence. That the decree was self-imposed didn't lessen its weight. A wife and children—a family of his own—was not in his future.

Were this woman and this baby God's way of compensating him for what he'd chosen to forego? He'd savor the crumbs like a starving man longing for a banquet. He filled the early morning hours thanking God for giving him these few short weeks to absorb a lifetime of memories. Memories he'd cherish when his life was once again barren and lonely.

Aaron swung the car into the mall parking lot hunting for a space close to the door. He drove up and down the crowded rows passing empty spots on the fringes of the lot.

Carrie shifted in her seat. "Park the car!"

He frowned. "Is it always this busy on Friday afternoons?" He turned the wheel and drove down the next aisle. A car pulled out. "This is what I want. We're close to the doors." Soon Benny was strapped into his lightweight-folding stroller. If Jason could see him now.

Carrie tugged at his shirtsleeve. "This way."

They entered the major department store through the women's department. Brushing past racks of slacks and blouses, they wound their way around the center escalator.

Aaron's feet slowed. *Oh boy.* Miles of lacy intimate apparel stretched out before him.

Carrie's chin lifted in a mutinous tilt. "I *told* you I wanted to shop by myself."

He clenched and unclenched his hands on the stroller's handles. "I'm not leaving you alone."

"Yes, you are. I want to...." Her words dried up, and she finished by waving her hand in the air.

Her blush delighted him.

Her chin hiked higher. "Fine, then. Follow me." She dove between racks loaded with frilly nightgowns.

He couldn't follow with the stroller. *Out-foxed.*

She maneuvered between the racks passing a sales woman helping a man in a tan trench coat.

Cooling his heels, Aaron watched her browse through several racks before, her color high and her eyes shooting little green darts, she made her way back to him.

Now what was she up to?

Hemmed in by nightgowns, she planted herself in front of him. "If you're staying, make yourself useful."

Without a lick of warning, she held out two—well, they were tops. That much he knew, but what they were called eluded him. He'd never stood this close to clothing with so much lace or with that many tiny buttons and bows.

"I can't decide which camisole to get. What do you think?"

Oh, lady. He was pretty sure he shouldn't *have* an opinion. His ears were about to catch on fire. He couldn't do this. *Give ground or fall in so deep you'll never find your way out, Black.* "You have exactly fifteen minutes to make your choice." Talking hurt his throat.

"I need thirty."

He glanced at the red lace she held in her right hand and the black lace she held in her left hand. "Thirty then. And don't leave this department."

"Where are you going?"

The hint of worry in her voice gave him a much-needed shot of satisfaction. "Tool department."

"Tools?"

"Yup. Guy stuff." *Boy, did he need to look at some guy stuff.* "Has Benny ever seen a hammer or a wrench?"

Her baffled look told him all he needed to know. "Didn't think so." He wheeled the stroller around. "Thirty minutes. The clock is ticking."

Carrie held the camisoles up. The black one with tiny decorative buttons down the front was her favorite. She glanced at Aaron's retreating back and for a moment wished he'd taken her up on the dare she'd thrown in his face and told her which one he liked. She shook her head at her own silliness. *Like I need the information for future reference?*

With no time to waste, she returned the impractical garments to the racks and went to find one a bit more sensible. Picking out several, she hurried to the dressing room.

Finding one that fit perfectly, she headed for the checkout counter. Appeasing the twinges of guilt over her treatment of Aaron, she waited for him as he'd asked. To pass the time she poked through the clearance rack.

"Carrie."

The smooth voice sent a jolt down her spine.

"Carrie."

Panic swept through her. Determined not to show fear, she clutched her shopping bag close and faced Ross. "What are you doing here?"

He smirked. "What do you think?" He stepped closer.

She backed away, shivering beneath his gaze.

"The guard dog finally left you alone."

"You were watching me?"

Ross's superior smile caused her stomach to roll. *Aaron, where are you?*

A man in a long coat stood in the next aisle going through a rack of bathrobes. The sales woman had disappeared.

"Where's my son?" Ross stepped closer. His smile didn't reach his eyes.

She backed away, desperate to see Aaron, and at the same time fearing what might happen if he showed up. "Leave me alone."

"Now you know I can't do that."

Behind Ross, an empty clothes rack swayed and crashed to the floor. He whirled around.

The man in the long coat struggled to right the rack. He fumbled it, causing the metal bar to bang against Ross's shins.

Ross's angry outcry released the fear paralyzing Carrie. She darted away between the racks of clothes. They rubbed against her as though clinging to her to hold her back. She tried to remember the way to the tool department, but in her panic got turned around. The escalator, filled with customers, glided up toward her. Several teens got off, jostling her aside. She glanced over her shoulder.

Ross moved toward her, a murderous rage burning in his eyes.

Shaking, she plunged headlong onto the escalator ignoring the indignant cries as she pushed her way through the crowd. For every step she took down, the escalator glided up—towards Ross.

Chapter Fourteen

"Com'on, buddy. Up we go." Aaron rolled the stroller onto the escalator and balanced the front wheels on a step. He was getting the hang of stroller maneuvers, popping a wheelie in the tool aisle. Not bad for a small rig that folded like an umbrella. Aaron leaned over between the handles. Big brown baby eyes gazed back at him. "What we could do in one of those fancy jobs, huh, Benny, my boy?"

Benny lifted his chin higher and smiled.

From Aaron's perspective, he'd never seen a more beautiful upside-down toothless grin. He grabbed one of the little hands reaching for him. "Maybe I can talk your mama into going out for an ice cream cone."

A shout followed by a grumbling murmur cut off Benny's chortle. The crowd at the top of the escalator jerked and heaved like a disorderly mob, before parting around a flying mass of red-gold hair.

Carrie. He'd know that head of hair anywhere. Why was she coming down the ascending escalator? The terror in her eyes set his heart pounding. He searched the crowd. "Carrie!" he shouted over the angry buzz of shoppers. Gripping Benny's stroller in one hand, he strong-armed the man in front of him. "I'm here. Let her through, people." He scanned the crowd at the top again, this time recognizing Ross.

"Aaron!" Carrie spotted him. "He's following me." Her words and tears parted a path through the people.

"I see him." He couldn't safely jockey the stroller through the crowd that had boarded behind him, and he didn't have time to take Benny out of the stroller and snap it shut. Taking Carrie's shopping bag, he tucked it in next to the baby. "Take over here." She stood on the step stiff with fear, so he placed her hands on the grips. "The minute we hit the top, you head for the nearest store."

"What will you do?" Her voice shook.

"Depends on him."

Ross stood at the top of the escalator, a smug sneer of his face as the moving stairway carried them closer.

In his peripheral vision, Aaron noted two security guards hustling toward the commotion. They were fresh-faced kids playing dress-up in spiffy uniforms and wide brimmed Mountie hats. A fight on their watch would be a big deal.

The people at the top of the escalator surged forward, hurrying to move out of harms way. Two women latched onto the guards talking and pointing at Carrie.

Two steps to go.

A man lurched past the escalator and fell against Ross, spilling an icy pink drink down the front of him.

Ross shrieked, and chaos broke out. People scattered before the running security guards.

Aaron bent over and flung his arm across the front of the stroller and Benny. "Let go, Carrie." He lifted the stroller, squealing baby and all, and balanced it on his hip.

His hand on her lower back, Aaron swept Carrie along at his side. "We're outta here."

"Did you see that?" She huffed, struggling to keep up with his running strides.

"Yeah. Hurry." He grabbed her hand and glanced down at Benny, snug and safe in the flying stroller. "Good thing we don't have a luxury model, 'eh kiddo?"

Oblivious to everything but the bumpy ride, Benny grinned and squealed.

"Right." Aaron glanced back. "Glad someone is getting a kick out of this."

"What?" Carrie gripped his hand harder.

"Nothing. Keep moving."

"Are they coming after us? Will they arrest me?" Her voice rose in panic.

"No and no." He veered into the food court and headed for the doors that led to the parking lot.

"I recognize that man." She puffed along behind him, clinging to his hand.

Aaron glanced around. "What man? And why does that matter *now*?"

"The man that spilled the Maui Wowie."

Slowing, Aaron pushed her ahead. "Hold the door so I can go through with the stroller." He'd chosen to leave by a different door than the one they came in. The car was parked around the corner.

"He's a horrible klutz." Carrie labored to catch her breath.

Aaron wanted to walk with the crowd, but Carrie's bright spill of hair made blending in impossible. *Best to hotfoot it out of here.*

"I'm surprised Ross can walk after getting bashed in the shins with that clothes rack."

Alarm shivered through Aaron. "You hit Ross with a clothes rack?" He should have never left her side.

"No! You're not listening to me."

They rounded the corner of the building. Aaron made a beeline for the car. "Unbuckle Benny while I unlock the car."

Together, they loaded Benny and the stroller in record time. Pulling out of the parking space, he drove away from the stores and toward the exit at the rear of the lot.

"Anyway, that man looks familiar." She opened the glove box and dug around. Finding a green ponytail holder that jingled, she wound it around her hair.

Distracted by traffic and what she was doing, Aaron asked, "What man?"

She *tsked* and shook her head. The little silver bells sewn onto the ponytail holder jingled.

Aaron grinned.

"What's so funny?" She sent him a withering look.

"Nothing. An angel just got her wings."

She huffed. "You're making no sense. That poor man is having a terrible day. I'm glad I'm not responsible for the cleaning bill on that tan trench coat."

Tan trench coat. He tried to recall where he'd seen someone wearing one. "How do you know him?"

"I don't *know him* know him. He was at the rack of robes just before—" Her voice broke, and she went silent.

An image of a man in a trench coat being helped by a sales woman flashed through Aaron's mind. He glanced at Carrie.

She gazed out the side window, gnawing on her knuckles, shock catching up with her.

"Tell me again about the empty rack."

She heaved a sigh. The tiny bells jingled merrily. "Are you listening this time?"

He let her peevishness go. He'd take that over tears. "Tell me every detail."

Her face clouded. "Ross showed up. He was spying on us. He knew you'd left me alone."

"A mistake I *will not* make again."

She fiddled with her bracelets. "He called you my guard dog."

Aaron snorted. A dog would have been a better companion for her today. A dog wouldn't have given a second thought to all the feminine frills and lace on display.

"He asked about Benny." To the accompaniment of a silvery tinkling, she shifted in her seat and checked Benny who was asleep in his car seat. "Aaron, I wanted you with me." A tear slid down her cheek.

He gulped. *Wouldn't you know she'd say that while they were in a moving car, and his hands were occupied with driving?*

"But at the same time, I was afraid you'd come and… and…."

Don't cry. Don't cry. Don't cry. He'd be in more trouble than he already was if she cried. "So what happened next?"

"The empty clothes rack behind Ross crashed to the ground. That man in the coat knocked it over. How does that even happen? So embarrassing."

How did it happen? Those things were heavy and not easily bumped over. He left the highway and got onto the streets of town.

"He felt terrible. He accidentally hit Ross with one of the bars."

Wondering about the accidental part, Aaron kept his mouth shut.

"That's all I saw. I ran after that."

He settled his hand over both of hers to stop her finger-twisting fidgets. "You did the right thing."

"I wanted to wait for you. To make up for," she shrugged,

"you know, what I did to you earlier." She hesitated a moment then whispered, "I'm sorry."

He tossed her a roguish grin and turned the car onto Margin Street. "You think you can say you're sorry, and I'll forgive you just like that?" The tiny bells were driving him crazy.

Her mouth dropped open as uncertainty flickered across her features.

"You owe me more than an 'I'm sorry.' Even one so nicely said."

"I do?"

"Yup." *Keep the conversation light, Black.* "I saved you from not only a raging Ross but also from a trench-coated bumbling fool armed with a Maui Owie." He took his eyes off the street for a moment and waggled his eyebrows at her.

She giggled. "A Maui *Wowie*."

"Whatever. The drink was pink and, therefore, lethal."

"I suppose I owe you a nice home cooked dinner."

Whoa! This was going better than expected. "That's a good start."

"A start?"

"Yes, and I accept the dinner invitation."

She frowned. "What else?"

He pulled the car into the driveway, shut off the engine, and swiveled toward her. "A kiss."

Her eyes grew round. "A kiss?"

"Mm-hmm."

Flustered, she fidgeted to a chorus of jingle bells. "When?"

"Right now."

"Here?" She looked at him as if he'd left his loose screws behind in the tool department.

He leaned close. "Right here. Right now."

Her eyes sparkled. "Okay." She crossed the small distance between them. Her soft lips lightly touched his.

A jolt of electricity hit him but without the pain. Only a pleasure so sweet he was sure, given half a chance, he could become addicted. Her scent, a mix of lemon and essence of Carrie, sent his thoughts spiraling.

She began to pull away.

Lifting his hand, he tangled his fingers in the hair at her nape, holding her still. With only a breath between his lips and hers, he whispered, "There's one more thing I want before your apology is complete."

"One more thing?" Her gaze drifted over his face.

"Yeah." He slid his hand through the luxurious length of her hair, snagging the jingling ponytail holder. Leaning away from her a smidge, he held it up in her line of vision. "This."

Confusion replaced the dreamy warmth in her eyes. "My ponytail holder?"

"Yeah." He smiled than planted a quick kiss on her moist lips. "Apology accepted."

Carrie leaned into the crib and gave Benny a kiss on his cheek. "Sweet dreams, puddin'." She closed the nursery door behind her and padded down the hall to her living room where Aaron sat sprawled on her couch. "I thought you'd left."

"We need to talk." His eyes followed her as she moved into the kitchen.

"I'm tired." She lifted a jug of iced tea from the fridge and turned around only to bump into a solid wall of muscled man.

"I want to take you some place safe while I figure out how to handle Ross."

Carrie ducked around him and took two glasses out of the

cupboard. "Ross is a control freak. I have to convince him he no longer has control of me."

"He's stalking you and he won't stop." He crossed his arms and braced his feet wide apart.

Her heart sank. Whatever it was he had to say, she wasn't going to like it. She set the glasses of iced tea aside. "What?"

He cocked his eyebrow in her direction.

She knew she sounded belligerent. *Big deal.* Her knees were still knocking from the mall episode.

"I'm a policeman."

She forced her gaping mouth closed. *Aaron. A cop. Standing in the middle of her kitchen.*

He held his hand out. "Come into the living room and sit with me."

She whacked his hand away. "No! I'm not going any place with you. Why didn't you tell me?" Angry tears burned her eyes.

"You never asked."

"But I told you how I felt...." Too upset to grasp the words she wanted to say, she stared at him.

He swiped a hand across his face. "Okay. I admit I should have told you sooner."

"Why didn't you?"

"Because you *need* me. I was afraid you'd react like this and kick me out." His features softened. "Please don't cry. You need me here, Carrie."

"I'm angry. I cry when I'm angry."

"When you're finished being angry, please let me explain why I'm so concerned."

She sniffed. He was about to weasel his way past all her indignation and her anger would just melt away. She wasn't ready to let it go. Not yet. She wanted to wallow in the fury and take all her frustration out on him because he was here and the creepy old boyfriend causing all the trouble, thankfully, wasn't.

She felt safe with Aaron. He was good and kind, and other than being stubborn and over protective, he hadn't done anything but, well, be there when she needed him. *Not the best reasoning if you're trying to stay angry, Carrie Anne.* She marched into the living room and flounced down onto the couch. "This better be good."

He sat opposite her on the edge of the overstuffed chair, his hands clasped between his knees. A crooked smile tipped his lips, threatening to dissolve the last bit of anger she clung to. She tried to scowl harder.

"You've already admitted he's prone to violence. You and Benny are in danger. Let me take you where you're safe while the local police diffuse the situation." Aaron rubbed the back of his neck. "Let me go to the police."

"No!" She took a breath, quelling her panic. "Ross said they would never believe anything I said about him." She shook her head. "The family practically owns the town. I could lose Benny."

"I find that hard to believe."

She had to make him believe her. "Are you from a small town?"

"No." He didn't meet her gaze. "Chicago."

She shoved aside her desire to continue the indulgent sniveling. He was hiding something. To get specific answers, her questions had to be carefully worded. "Why are you here? And don't tell me you're on vacation."

He leaned his head back to rest against the lace antimacassar and closed his eyes.

Was he trying to think of a plausible story? She dismissed that notion. Aaron was truthful, but he never said more than necessary.

"I'm on a leave of absence."

In the kitchen the refrigerator hummed.

"Why?" She needed him to be more specific. "What happened?"

He seemed to shrink back. Carrie blinked but the impression didn't leave her.

"I messed up big time." A self-deprecation twisted his lips. "I shouldn't admit that when I'm demanding you trust my judgment."

She didn't dare speak.

He drummed his fingers on the arm of the overstuffed chair. "We were working a drug sting." Absentmindedly, he pulled on a thread trailing from the fabric and twisted it around his finger. His eyes lost focus.

Carrie sat quietly, afraid to breathe lest she distract him from finishing the story. His finger worked the loose thread. She'd let him unravel the entire chair if that helped him tell his story.

"The deal was to go down in a machine shop. I waited high on a catwalk next to my partner, providing cover in case the dealer brought in backup." He growled in disgust. "Would've been better if he had." He shook his head, horror in his eyes. "The sleazebag brought his woman and her infant. A baby at a drug deal! That changed everything. If the baby got hit with a stray bullet...." The mere possibility put a strain in his voice.

"What happened?" Carrie couldn't tell if he heard her whispered question.

He continued to fiddle with the thread. "I wore a headset. The chief told me to leave the catwalk. My new assignment was to extract the infant if the deal went sour. I used machinery as cover and got in close." His lips flattened into a grim line. "The building presented us with a security risk

135

from the beginning. The overhead doors on the loading dock were wide open." He inhaled. The next words flew out with a rush of air. "A rival gang heard about the deal and wanted in on the action. They came in through those doors."

Carrie slipped off the couch and knelt beside his chair, resting her hand on his forearm.

"The woman set the baby on a pile of tarps." He cleared his throat. "I don't know who let loose first. I heard the shots on the other side of the building. I'd run out of time. Bullets were ricocheting off the machinery. I grabbed the baby." The thread between his fingers snapped. He raised shaking hands to his face. "I remember an explosion. The repercussion slammed me into the metal framework of a huge lathe." His voice grew hoarse. "Next thing I remember I was on a gurney riding in an ambulance."

He paused, and Carrie remained quiet, letting him gather his thoughts.

"A stray bullet hit a drum of old chemicals and caused the explosion." He rubbed his face. "They eventually told me the baby died in my arms when we were body slammed against the lathe." His chest rose and fell as he struggled to regain control of his emotions.

Taking his hand, Carrie laced her fingers between his. This explained so much that puzzled her. His initial fear of holding Benny. His over-protectiveness. His determination not to fail at keeping them safe. "Aaron, you did your best. You couldn't have prevented the explosion."

He swallowed hard.

She squeezed his hand. "Even when horrible things happen to us, God is present and in control." The haunted look in Aaron's eyes tore at her heart.

"She was a baby. Why'd God let that happen to her?"

"I don't know. Nobody but God can answer that question."

"Maybe God expected me to save her and I didn't act soon enough." His voice shook.

She gripped his hand so hard her fingers hurt. "What happened that night did not surprise God. He knew before you ever stepped foot into that building exactly what would take place. Why He allowed it to happen is beyond our understanding. We can try and comfort ourselves with guesses and speculation, but we will never know the mind of God."

He pinched the bridge of his nose between thumb and forefinger in a vain attempt to stop the tears that trickled down his cheeks and dripped off his chin. "Why doesn't He prove His power over evil?"

Carrie smiled and whispered. "He already did that, Aaron. Two thousand years ago on Resurrection morning." She shifted her weight. Her knees were numb from kneeling too long in one position. "God never promised an easy life. He never even promised life would make sense. He *did* promise he'd be with us through the ordeals and the suffering."

A watery grin tipped the corners of his lips. "You're talking like my grandmother. Right about now she'd be quoting scripture." Eyes bright with tears, he wrapped a red gold curl around his finger. "How'd you get so smart?"

"Not long ago I had this same conversation with Pastor Peter." She swept her free hand across his chin, catching a tear that lingered there. "Knowing this doesn't make life any easier. We want to be in control. Instead, we have to trust Some One we can't see. That's hard to do." She leaned closer and whispered, "Especially if we lose touch with Him."

He chuckled. "I promise I'll do better at attending church." With his free hand, he crossed his heart before pulling their entwined fingers to his mouth and brushing his lips across her knuckles. "Promise. And you have to promise me something in return."

She tried to answer, but her heart fluttered in her throat so she nodded.

"Let me take you and Benny someplace safe."

Burt tossed his sticky coat into the backseat of the car, slammed the door, and climbed into the driver's seat. As days went in this business, today was a bust. He'd lost his anonymity and the biker guy had an eye on his car. Time to make some changes.

Fishing his keys out of his pocket, he started the engine. He didn't like surprises, and he'd had too many on this job. He pulled onto the highway headed inland, away from the coast. Away from the small town where everyone knew too much of everyone else's business. First stop—the dry cleaners followed by a few others, and he'd be back in business.

Chapter Fifteen

She walked toward him glowing with happiness, carrying her baby. He reached for her in anticipation. She came closer and her smile turned to a grimace. A bright light surrounded her, washing the color from her skin, her hair, and her clothing. A pale shadow of herself she held the baby out to him. "Take him. Save him."

Her voice sent shivers through him. He wouldn't leave her. He could save both of them if she listened to him. He took the child in his arms, but she began to fade. Her cry hurt his ears. He wanted to clap his hands over them, but if he did that he'd drop the baby.

Heart pounding Aaron awoke, his face and shoulders wet. He dug under his pillow to grab the buzzing phone.

"Black."

A pause was followed by Jason's voice heavy with disbelief. "You sleeping?"

Aaron ran a hand over his face and stared at his wet palm. "Yeah."

"Why? Something happen last night?"

Jason's sharp tone cut through the remnants of sleep and

the nightmarish dream. Aaron checked his watch. Ten o'clock on a Saturday morning. He leaped out of bed. A gust of wind blew in through the open window at the head of the bed bringing with it a spattering of much needed rain.

He scrambled to close the window, trying to remember the last time he'd paid attention to the weather forecast.

"What's happening out there?" Impatience laced Jason's voice. "Talk to me."

A shaky laugh escaped Aaron's lips. "It's raining."

"You're in bed at this hour because of *rain*?"

"No, I'm soaking wet because of the rain. But you didn't call to talk about the weather. Do you have anything on the registration I gave you?"

"The car's rented to a corporation, Baggi, Limited. Before you ask, they're a big importer and distributor of women's handbags. High end stuff."

"Pocketbooks?" Aaron sank down on the damp sheets. "That driver isn't selling purses."

"I'll dig deeper."

"Hold off on that." Aaron drew in a deep breath. "I need your help here." He filled his friend in on what transpired at the mall. "Ross has her convinced if she goes to the police, she'll lose her baby." His heart ached knowing she'd suffered at the hands of Ross and hadn't dared turn to anyone for help. "I want her out of this town. I'll call our chief and ask what he knows about this place. See if that's true or just a line fed to her by an abuser."

"She okay about leaving?" Jason asked.

Aaron snorted. "She told me she'd think about it and let me know."

"And one way or another, you will be sure her answer is yes?"

"More like, 'Yes, and I'll be ready to leave first thing

tomorrow morning.'" Jason's sharp bark of laughter hurt Aaron's ear.

"Okay. I'll leave within the hour. Secure your bike," Jason said.

"She probably won't pack light."

Jason chuckled. "I've got a cap on the bed of the truck. Have her and the baby ready to travel."

"Thanks." Aaron ended the call and tossed his phone on the dresser. He felt more rested than he had in weeks, even after waking from that horrible dream. Last night, after talking to Carrie about the bungled mission, the knot he'd carried in his chest had finished unraveling. The ache had been a part of him for so long, he felt hollow without it. Heading to the bathroom, he looked out the window. The sedan was gone.

Trying to puzzle out the connection between the generic car rental and an importer of expensive handbags, he turned on the hot water and stepped into the shower.

Aaron sprinted across the driveway. Anger and panic warred for space in his chest. Her gray station wagon wasn't in the driveway. She hadn't left him a note.

He thundered up the steps and banged on the purple door. "Thelma?" He pounded again. "Thelma!"

Over the *rat-tat-tat* of rain, he heard her call out. He waited impatiently for her to unlock the door. At least she remembered to lock it.

Dressed in a purple sweat suit, Thelma opened the door. She held Benny on one hip. "What's wrong?"

"Where's Carrie?"

"She's at the beach."

"In this weather?" He fought to gain control of his seesawing emotions.

"Well, yes." Thelma backed away as Aaron stepped over the threshold. "There's nothing more beautiful than the surf in a storm."

"Is she alone?"

Benny fussed and squirmed in Thelma's arms. "She needed time to think."

Aaron let go of the breath he hadn't realized he was holding. She promised to think about his proposal. Why couldn't she have done her thinking in the safety of her apartment?

Thelma's troubled gaze held his. "She said you want to take her and the baby away from here. Where will you go?"

"Chicago."

A mixture of fear and sadness crossed Thelma's lined face.

Impatient to find Carrie, he said, "Why don't you come along?" *What are you doing, Black? An elderly woman will slow you down.*

"Me? You want me to go?"

He plowed ahead, wondering about his sanity. "You could help Carrie with the baby." *And maybe if she knows you're going, she'll say yes.* "She'll be more comfortable if you are there."

Thelma nodded. "I'll chaperone."

Alrighty then. He needed to work on his reputation. "I have a friend coming for us. He has a truck with a double cab."

She frowned, deepening the wrinkles across her brow.

"The truck has a back seat."

"Oh." Thelma's confusion cleared. "You'd better go get her. I'll pack." Talking softly to Benny, Thelma bustled away.

Aaron bypassed the steps and leapt off the porch. He didn't have time to haul on raingear. He hopped on his bike and sped toward the coast, dodging the largest puddles and praying.

Carrie's old gray wagon was parked in the lot at the jetty.

Aaron's blood ran cold. Beside it sat the black SUV. A dark expletive ground out between his teeth as he parked his bike and climbed onto the rocks.

Carrie stood at the end of the jetty surrounded by a foaming expanse of gunmetal gray water.

Aaron's breath caught in his throat when he recognized the man making his way across the uneven rocks toward her.

Ross.

The wind and rain buffeted them, whipping their hair and pulling at their clothes. Huge waves broke against the rocks. Spray exploded into the air.

Engrossed in the magnificent display of nature's power, Carrie remained unaware of Ross's presence.

A deadly calm born of desperation held Aaron in its grip. He couldn't warn her. She wouldn't hear him over the crash of the waves and the howl of the wind. Leaping over the gaping cracks between boulders, Aaron moved across the wet rocks. He didn't have a crowd to disappear into this time. Only the three of them were on the rocks.

And God.

The thought jerked him to a halt. *Yeah. And God.* He shifted his focus to Carrie.

Hair hanging in damp clumps, she turned and spotted Ross. Fear distorted her pale face.

Hoping God really was present Aaron whispered, "Lord, you're all we have." He scrambled faster, close enough now to hear Ross's voice as he yelled at Carrie and waved his arms.

Carrie stepped back, causing Aaron's heart to stutter. She balanced on the edge of a rock slick with seaweed. "Dear Lord, no." She spotted him. Her lips moved, saying his name.

Ross glanced over his shoulder and speared Aaron with hostile eyes. Face red with fury, he lunged for Carrie.

She stepped back. Her arms wind milled.

"No!" Horror distorted time to slow motion as Aaron scrambled over the rocks.

A huge wave swelled and crashed over Carrie, pulling her into the heaving ocean.

Ignoring the urge to wipe the shock off Ross's pretty-boy face, Aaron slid down the rocks and crouched on a partially submerged boulder. Icy cold salt water swirled around his knees.

Carrie's head popped out of the white foam.

His heart raced at the sight of her.

She gasped for air, and the water pulled her under again.

Aaron plunged in after her. Ross's voice calling out to Carrie was the last thing he heard as the cold water closed around him.

A violent backwash at the base of the jetty threatened to pound him against the rocks. He pushed away from them with his feet, thankful he still wore his boots.

Sand from the ocean's floor swirled through the turbulent water, rough against his skin. He surfaced, and over his own heaving breath, he heard a gurgling sputter.

A foaming wave pulled Carrie away from the rocks before dragging her under.

Diving after her, his searching hand caught in a swirling silken mass. He tightened his fingers hoping—praying—she lived to ream him out for yanking her up by the hair. Hooking his other arm around her, he pulled her to the surface.

Panicked, she grabbed for his head. Her breath whistled in his ear.

To stop her from drowning both of them, he tucked his chin and grasped her forearms. He pushed her up and away from him. Fighting the water and her, he flipped her on her back. He flung his arm across her, anchoring her to him.

A spiller wave crashed over them, driving them against the rocks.

Aaron took the brunt of the impact against his back and shoulders. He ignored the rough bite of barnacles and the sting of salt as the sucking water pulled them down into a trough. Carrie's fingers dug into his arm. He surfaced and inhaled before being pulled under again.

Towering crests from opposing waves collided overhead. His breath burned in his lungs as he fought to hold onto Carrie. Floundering in cross-seas, desperation boiled through him. *God, help us.* This time, his strength and cunning weren't enough to save them. With everything in him, he reached out to God. No words. Only a yearning so urgent and deep it sent sharp pains through his chest as if his lungs and his heart were cracking open.

In a swift, uplifting surge, pressure pushed hard against Aaron's back and hips. His senses spun as the water swirled across him, the force never letting up. He pulled Carrie closer, afraid she'd be ripped from his arms as they rose higher and higher on a giant rogue wave. His head broke the surface. They were headed straight for the jetty.

He closed his eyes and tensed, bracing for the pain when they were dashed against the rocks. The impact would be a bone breaker. *Carrie needs to live for Benny.* He opened his eyes. They were above the jetty. He kicked his feet and cracked his knee against a rock. Then, incredibly, gently, the monster wave rolled out from under them, leaving them high on the rocks.

Aaron lay on his back staring at the dark, roiling clouds. Raindrops pelted his face. Carrie lay draped across his chest, wheezing and gagging.

What just happened? His chest rose and fell as he coughed and gasped, pulling in air as fast as his hurting lungs allowed.

Carrie rose on one elbow and pushed away from him, rolling so her head hung over a yawning crevice between the rocks. At her first gut-twisting retch, Aaron, still hacking up the water he'd sucked in, shifted closer to her and pulled her tangled hair away from her face. When she finished, he gathered her close and held her, savoring they were alive and in one piece. "I'd offer you my t-shirt, but it won't help."

Nestled in his arms, Carrie's teeth chattered. "Th-thank you for saving me."

He squeezed her shoulders. "Don't thank me. I didn't pull us out of that mess." Pausing, he studied the churning water. "God did."

Her smile wobbled, a watery shadow of its usual self. She whispered, "You're right. Thank you, God."

"Really, Carrie—" A severe spasm of coughing stopped him. He leaned over the edge of the rock and cleared the water from his aching lungs. Her small hand felt good rubbing his back. Able to speak once more he said, "What happened was a miracle, Carrie."

She stared at him for a moment. "Without you I would've drowned."

He shook his head. "This time your survival wasn't my doing."

146

She frowned and rubbed the top of her head. "You pulled my hair."

Aaron settled her against his chest. "Listen to me. A monster wave picked us up and set us pretty as you please right here on this rock."

"What are you saying?"

"I can't explain it other than a pressure against my back, lifting us up. I thought for sure when we hit the rocks we'd break bones, maybe crash to our death." He shook his head in wonder. "What happened is a real miracle."

"It *was* a big wave," she agreed.

"Yup." He gave her a peck on the top of her wet head, tasting salt on his lips. "And an unseen hand lifted us and set us this rock. I know my abilities, Carrie, and I'd hit the end of my resources." He paused. "I thought you believed in miracles."

She frowned. "I do. You don't."

Grinning, he hugged her close and helped her up. She'd lost a sneaker, and her bare foot was scraped and raw. Ross was no longer on the rainy, windswept jetty. "What did Ross say to you?"

"He wants a family." She paused. "He was surprised Benny wasn't with me."

Alarm rippled through Aaron. "Does he know Benny is with Thelma?"

"I didn't tell him." Her eyes widened. "Do you think...?"

"Let's go." Afraid she'd fall in a crevice, he stayed close helping her cross the uneven rocks. "I'm driving you home."

He loaded her in the car and buckled her seat belt all the time fearing that Ross was way ahead of them. If he knocked on Thelma's door, and she answered holding Benny.... A chill prickled along Aaron's spine.

Racing for home, he took every shortcut he knew.

Turning onto Margin Street, he cut the corner narrowly missing an oncoming car.

Ross's SUV was parked at the curb.

Carrie shivered, clutching her hands together on her lap. She stared straight ahead, lips moving in silent prayer.

"Hang on." Stomping the gas pedal, Aaron bore down on the SUV. But before they got close, Ross pulled away from the curb with tires squealing.

Aaron shot into the driveway on an angle. The car bumped across Thelma's lawn. At the foot of the front steps, he jammed on the brakes, throwing them forward in their seatbelts. He leapt from the car and raced up the steps. His feet hit the porch just as the purple door opened.

Thelma stood before him holding Benny in her arms. "Did you find her?"

Relief washed through Aaron. Knees weak, he leaned against the porch railing.

Carrie climbed the steps, breathing hard and coughing. "Auntie. Thank God you and Benny are okay."

"Of course we are." Thelma's gaze darted back and forth from Carrie to Aaron. "What happened to you two?"

Aaron helped Carrie up the last two steps. He'd let her explain to Thelma. He just wanted to stare at her. She wore one shoe. Her hair hung in wet hanks. Her clothes were soaked with seawater, and she looked beautiful to him. *Thank you, God.*

Dressed in sweats, Carrie reclined on her couch bundled in a blanket. Aunt Thelma had insisted on following her home to supervise her recovery from her dunk in the ocean. A hot shower helped, but she couldn't stop shivering. If she closed her eyes she still felt the sensation of water rolling over her, pressing her down.

Aaron knelt beside the couch. Raindrops glistened in his short hair. Wet spatter marks marked his dry t-shirt. The dark circles under his eyes gave him a haunted look. Lines of worry bracketed his mouth.

"How are you doing?" His eyes roved over her.

"Okay. You?"

His lips tipped in a tight smile. "I've been better."

"Got your bike?"

"Yeah. Mr. Beedle was pleased Thelma called him to take me back to the beach. How's your foot?"

She pushed it out from under the blanket so he could see how Thelma had wrapped it in gauze. "Stings a little."

"We'll keep an eye on it." He covered a yawn and rubbed his hand over his face.

Carrie's chest tightened. He'd depleted his incredible strength. He'd proven he'd take any risk to protect her. A lump rose in her throat. If he'd drowned it would've been because of her. A sob escaped her lips.

He sat on the couch next to her and wrapped his arms around her. Giving into the comfort and warmth of his embrace, she held onto him until the tears stopped. She blew her nose on the tissue he offered. "I cry an awful lot around you."

He smiled. "I have a way with women." He rose and pulled the coffee table closer before sitting on it to face her. "I've talked to Jason. He'll be here in the morning."

Thelma entered the room carrying a tray loaded with sandwiches and hot tea. "Both of you missed lunch. Eat up." She placed the tray on the table beside Aaron and went to check on Benny napping in his crib.

Carrie took the tuna salad sandwich Aaron offered her.

She knew he was waiting for her to say she'd leave her home and go into hiding.

She studied him as he wolfed down his sandwich. She didn't like the idea of leaving her apartment and job, but she couldn't expect him to keep rescuing her. Taking a sip of hot tea to sooth her throat, she asked, "How long would I be gone?"

Hope lit his eyes and tugged at her heartstrings. "I won't lie to you, Carrie. I don't know. But Thelma has agreed to go with us."

"She has?"

"She can help you care for Benny."

"There's so much to do. I need to pack and notify the Neighborhood Center and the church. Everyone would worry if I just left without a word." Her voice rose. "And there's food in the fridge that will spoil, and what about my mail?"

He took her plate from her and wrapped her cold hands in the warmth of his. "I spoke to Mr. Beedle on the ride. I told him what happened. He also thinks you should leave. He said he'd take care of your mail, houseplants, and anything else you can think of."

"And what about Thelma's apartment?"

"Thelma has contacted Pauline." He squeezed her hands as if afraid she'd disappear.

"Okay."

He looked at her closely. "Okay what?"

"Okay, I'll go."

The lines in his face relaxed. The kiss he placed on the back of her hand caused her heart to bump. His eyes were dark with tenderness. "Rest and then you can pack. You don't need to bring a lot."

Carrie smiled. "You're traveling with two women and a baby. Expect a lot."

Chapter Sixteen

Carrie stood at the stove tending sizzling bacon. Normally at this time she'd be getting ready for church. But early this morning before the sun came up, Aaron's friend, Jason, had arrived in his pickup truck. She'd watched through her curtains as a tall shadowy figure greeted Aaron with a one armed hug and a thump on the back.

She glanced at her clock and hurried to pour orange juice in glasses. Wanting to use the food in the fridge, she'd promised Aaron a big breakfast before hitting the road.

Thelma bustled through the kitchen door carrying an old carpetbag. "Good morning. Do I smell French toast?"

Carrie pointed at the oven. "Baked French toast."

In the nursery Benny cried.

"I'll get him." Thelma left the kitchen, calling out to the baby as she went.

The tread of feet on the stairs shook the flamingos on Carrie's shelf. She pressed a fist to her stomach to calm the flittering butterflies. Skirting a pile of luggage, she answered the knock on her door.

"Morning." Aaron kissed her on the cheek. "I'd like you to meet Jason Cooper."

Flustered by the kiss, Carrie held out her hand to the other man. "Thank you for coming." Long fingers engulfed her hand.

"You're welcome. Glad I can help." Jason stood a head taller than Aaron. He had a lean face and hard eyes.

Aaron toed the assorted gear stacked at her feet. "What's burning?"

Dropping her gracious hostess decorum, Carrie turned to make a mad dash to the kitchen and tripped over a tote filled with baby formula. Jason caught her elbow, keeping her from landing in a heap on the rug. Heat flamed across her cheeks. "Thank you."

His eyes twinkled though he didn't crack a smile. "You're welcome."

Mortified by her clumsiness, she scuttled away to save the bacon from becoming charcoal. Setting the food on the table she called everyone to the kitchen.

"Smells good." Aaron carried Benny much to Carrie's surprise. He set the baby in his carrier at the end of the table while Jason and Thelma found their seats.

After Carrie was seated, Aaron took his place. He held her hand, eyes serious. "I'd like to say grace this morning."

She stared at him, mouth gaping. Lacking words, she nodded and bowed her head.

"Father, thank you for the safe arrival of Jason. We ask for wisdom and protection as we travel. Bless the food and the hands that prepared it. Amen."

Carrie scrunched her eyes closed. Aaron's praying voice brought tears to her eyes. She wished she could listen to him pray everyday for the rest of her life. *Do* not *go there, Carrie*

Anne. To distract herself, she began to serve the baked French toast.

"Everything?" Aaron scrutinized the pile of suitcases and totes as though they hid a nest of snakes. He held up a folding stepstool. "Why do we need this?"

"Thelma needs it to climb in and out of the truck." Carrie set it back on the pile.

Jason picked up a tote filled with half the medicine cabinet. "Planning on getting sick?"

"I'm prepared. There's baby aspirin, cough syrup, a thermometer, ointment for diaper rash—"

He held up both hands in surrender. "Okay, okay. Mother knows best."

Thelma entered the room, wiping her hands on a kitchen towel. "The dishes are done. I left a few things on my porch that need to go into the truck."

With resignation, the men began hauling stuff to the truck.

Standing at the window holding Benny, sadness settled in Carrie's heart. For the first time in her life, she'd found a place that felt like home and now she was leaving.

Mr. Hickum toddled out to retrieve his morning paper. Across the street, Mr. Santana worked in his small rose garden. Someone had bought a new car. A white sedan was parked under the maple tree. Carrie loved this neighborhood and even knowing she was coming back, leaving was hard.

The men tramped in for another load. Aaron pointed at a bed pillow. "Why?" He shook his head. "Never mind." He exited the apartment carrying two suitcases with the pillow stuffed under his arm.

Jason snagged the bags closest to the door. One foot over the threshold, a faint chime jingled. Digging in a side pocket of the diaper bag, he pulled out Carrie's phone and held it up for her to see.

Panic swept through her. *Ross.*

Jason's eyes narrowed.

Shock jolted through Carrie as he answered the call.

"Hello. Hello?" He listened for a moment then disconnected.

"That's *my* phone." Carrie's indignation was tempered by the icy fear trickling through her.

"No one on the other end." He tucked it into the pocket and without a backward glance headed for the truck.

Carrie looked at Thelma. "This will be an interesting trip."

Aaron placed totes on the tailgate and waited for Jason to climb into the bed of the truck before pushing the totes to him. "She told me to expect this much stuff."

Jason crouched on all fours beneath the cap, arranging gear so it wouldn't shift while on the road. "Got your things packed?"

"Right here." Aaron pushed his duffle closer to Jason. "So what do you think?"

Pausing, Jason looked at Aaron. "You've got your hands full."

"Yeah." Aaron grinned.

"I don't see the car I traced on the street."

Aaron shook his head. "It's not here this morning." He should be pleased, but instead the absence worried him.

"Carrie just got a call." Jason hooked a bungee cord to

the bed of the truck and stretched it around the cooler to hold it in place.

The tone of his friend's voice captured Aaron's attention. "From who?"

"Don't know. Hung up."

"You listened?"

"I answered." Jason glanced at Aaron. "She didn't much care for that. I think she recognized the number."

Uneasy, Aaron's gaze traveled to the end of the street. "It's time to leave."

"You think it was the boyfriend?"

"Ex-boyfriend. That guy is off."

"Unglued?" Jason asked.

"Pretty much."

Jason hopped out of the truck. "I'll get Thelma's things." He flashed a sympathetic grin in Aaron's direction. "I'm leaving the women and baby in your hands."

Aaron grinned and headed indoors to round everyone up.

"Com'on Carrie. You've checked the locks on the windows four times." He cupped her elbow and guided her out the front door and locked it behind them. "You'll come back."

Jason helped Thelma into the back of the cab and handed her the huge purse she insisted on carrying. Snapping the stool closed, he slipped it behind the seat.

Helping Carrie in with Benny, Aaron spotted the dark SUV headed their way. "Let's get out of here."

Jason climbed behind the wheel. The truck was moving before Aaron finished climbing in. The truck tires dug into gravel, and they careened out of the driveway toward the highway.

In the backseat the women squealed.

Carrie finished securing Benny in his seat. She poked Aaron's shoulder. "Tell him to slow down!"

"Hang on." Jason pressed the gas pedal harder. "He's turning around and coming back."

"Who?" Carrie scooted forward on the seat. "Aaron, who?"

"Ross."

For the one hundred and fiftieth time, Carrie looked out the back windshield to try and spot Ross.

The men were murmuring back and forth in the front seat as Aaron gave cryptic directions to Jason. They wove through the side streets at an illegal speed before coming out on a busy road near the highway. They'd traveled through neighborhoods Carrie didn't know existed.

Thelma clutched her purse with both hands. Her eyes were closed, and her lips were moving in silent prayer.

Jason pulled onto the Interstate and sped up. Both men continued to check the mirrors and the vehicles traveling the road.

Carrie slipped a pacifier between Benny's lips. Closing her eyes, she sent prayers of her own heavenward. Soon the movement of the truck lulled her to sleep.

Carrie jerked awake as the truck slowed and pulled into a rest area.

On the other side of Benny's car seat, Thelma twisted about looking out the windows in all directions. With discreet hand gestures she tried to convey a message to Carrie.

Puzzled, Carrie shook her head.

"Pit stop." Aaron bailed out and helped Carrie with Benny while Jason did the same for Thelma.

At the restroom entrance, Aaron handed Carrie the diaper bag. "Make it snappy."

His boorish attitude raised her hackles, but Thelma grabbed her arm and pulled her into the ladies room before Carrie could respond in kind.

"Something is wrong," Thelma whispered.

Heart sinking toward her toes, Carrie set the diaper bag on the changing counter. They were getting out of town, hoping that things would change for the better. "What?"

"The men are talking low and watching our backs." Thelma loved to watch the crime shows on the television.

"Hurry up in there." Aaron's voice echoed through the concrete room.

Thelma held Benny. "You first, then you can finish changing him while I take my turn."

"But...."

Thelma clamped her red lips together and shooed Carrie on her way.

Juggling the baby between them, they finished in record time. Packing away the changing pad, Carrie whispered to Thelma. "Is Ross following us?"

The older woman leaned close. "I think that's what I heard them say. And call me crazy, but I think there's also a second car on our tail." Thelma's eyes gleamed. "I feel like I stepped into a movie—except it's real."

Carrie's heart hammered. It was all too real for her comfort.

"Hurry, ladies." Jason waited for them on the other side of the door, his impatience palpable.

She followed Thelma out of the building and into the warm sunshine. Aaron waited beside the truck. All business, he secured Benny in his seat and helped Carrie settle beside him.

The men traded places, giving Aaron a turn behind the wheel. Gunning the engine, he pulled into the traffic.

Fear curled in the pit of Carrie's stomach. She prodded Jason's shoulder. "What's happening? Is Ross following us?"

The men exchanged a look before Aaron glanced in the mirror at Carrie. "Yes, he is." He focused his attention back on the road and driving.

She felt fear stab through her all the way down to her toes. "And is there a second car, too?"

Jason twisted around to stare at Carrie with such intensity she fought the urge to check her face for smudges of dirt.

"Maybe." He turned away to watch the reflection in the side mirror.

His dismissal grated across her nerves. "Well, thanks for the clarification." *Sheesh.* She bit her tongue, keeping the rest of what she wanted to say to herself.

Jason was helping Aaron on her behalf. *Be thankful, Carrie.*

Carrie jiggled Benny's car seat. He'd squalled unhappily through lunch at a fast food joint. After the meal, Thelma had gone to the ladies room to reapply her makeup. Jason was hustling her along now. Her faded blue eyes above heavily rouged cheeks were snapping with fire. "I can move only so fast, young man."

Hand extended, waiting for her to accept his help getting into the truck, Jason didn't reply.

She tossed her big purse onto the seat and with his help, climbed in. "And next time you boys are planning a getaway, use a car." She settled in like a ruffled hen.

A ghost of a smile played across Jason's lips as he swung the truck's door closed and walked around to the driver's side to take over the next leg of the journey.

Tired, Carrie covered a noisy yawn.

Aaron swiveled around and smiled. The first smile she'd seen all day. "We'll stop for the night around supper time and finish the trip tomorrow."

Jason shot him a look that Carrie couldn't interpret, but she got the impression they disagreed about something. Neither one said anything more about the situation, so she settled down and played a game of peek-a-boo with Benny.

Dressed in a polo shirt and rumpled khakis, Burt sucked on the straw buried deep in a milkshake. Here was another thing he no longer liked about his job. Eating on the run made for lousy digestion. He drove a newer model car, which helped his attitude a little.

In a parking lot across the street, the little group prepared to leave. The old woman slowed them down. That worked for Burt. He pulled onto the highway a couple of cars behind them, and immediately began looking for an opening to move ahead of them.

He'd continue to alternate driving ahead of them on long stretches without exits and behind them when they might leave the highway. The way the two men were driving, they knew someone trailed them. He hoped their focus was on the dark SUV shadowing them so they would miss his maneuvering. Didn't matter either way. A showdown was near. He could feel it in his bones.

Chapter Seventeen

Carrie didn't have the makings of a good criminal. They were at the end of only the first day of travel, and she was already sick of being on the run.

The men pushed all afternoon, stopping only once after lunch. Everyone was irritable including Benny. No matter how many silly faces Mommy made, or how many songs Auntie sang, he was not happy. He was done with the car seat.

Night fell before they checked into a motel off the four-lane road. Built in the 1960s, the one-story building sprawled close to a highway that had been widened several times. Only a narrow shoulder separated the busy road and the narrow parking lot.

Aaron keyed the lock on the room she and Benny would share with Thelma. A 1960's color palette dominated the decor. A burnt orange shag carpet showed patches of wear. A pea green couch sloped as though someone had shortened the legs on one side. The bathroom wallpaper sported huge psychedelic flowers in yellow and peach. A watermark stained the ceiling in one corner.

Aaron dumped his duffel and assorted totes on the floor before he unlocked the connecting door to the neighboring room.

Jason stepped through the connecting door and looked around. "Your décor matches ours. Very retro."

Carrie caught a glimpse of a rare smile and thought he should do it more often.

In the bathroom, Thelma sprayed cleaner and swished and swiped all the time talking to no one in particular. Evidently, cleaning products were included in the contents of that oversized purse.

Flipping back a corner of the bedspread, Carrie ran a hand over the dingy linen. "The sheets feel clean." She created a nest for Benny in the center of the bed.

Aaron closed the drapes before rooting around in his duffel bag. "Stay here. Jason will rustle up supper while I check out the lay of the land around the hotel. Don't answer the door for anyone. Got it?"

Exhausted, Carrie sank to the edge of the couch. "Just feed me, please."

He locked Carrie's door and followed Jason through the connecting door and into the room they would use. She heard him rattle the knob to check that their door locked behind them as they left to get supper and check the area.

Thelma came to the bathroom door wielding a bottle of foaming aerosol cleaner and a wet cloth. "I'm cleaning the tub." She ducked back into the bathroom leaving Carrie wondering where her friend found all her energy.

Benny fussed and kicked at his blanket.

"I know, sweetie. You need changing. Give me a minute to find the diapers." Setting aside the worrisome thoughts that had plagued her while on the road, she sorted through the various totes. Taking a step back, she stumbled over Aaron's open duffel.

Something inside jingled.

Puzzled, Carrie nudged the duffle with her toe. The jingle intrigued her. *Probably pocket change.* She returned to searching for the pack of diapers.

Pocket change would be in his pocket.

Her curiosity piqued, she returned to Aaron's duffle. Grasping one end, she shook it setting off the soft jingling again.

Squatting, she lifted the open edge of the zipper and peeked inside at the assortment of clothing and a pair of boots. She lifted the boots. They were heavy and worn at the heels, and they fascinated her. The left one jingled.

Slipping her hand into the smooth interior, her fingers tangled in a wad of soft fabric. She withdrew her hand and sat with a thump on the cruddy carpet.

Ponytail holders. More than a dozen of them—and they were all hers.

Carrie dropped them on her lap. Tipping the boot upside down, she shook it. More bits of stretchy fabric poured out. Why was Aaron hoarding her ponytail holders? She fingered the red one with jingle bells, the one he'd taken from her hair.

She lost them left and right and had wondered why she wasn't finding them as she usually did. Her supply was low, and now she knew why. *The thief!* He should have given them back to her.

Thelma dropped something in the bath startling Carrie. Afraid she'd get caught riffling through Aaron's things, she stuffed the ponytail holders back in the boot and placed the boots in the duffle. She needed time to think about her discovery and what it meant.

By the time she finished searching the remaining totes for diapers, Benny had worked himself into a snit. Thelma walked into the room holding a squeeze bottle of tub cleaner.

Exasperated, Carrie picked up Benny. Using one hand, she went back through the totes she'd already searched. "They must be in a bag in the truck."

"What about his diaper bag?"

"I used the last one at the pit stop after lunch." She yelled to be heard over Benny's infuriated cries.

A muted crash came from the room next door.

Relief flooded through Carrie. The men were back. She pushed the adjoining door open. "Aaron? We need—" Her heart bounced into her throat, cutting off her words.

Ross stood in the center of the room, disheveled and breathing hard. His eyes shifted from corner to corner, a look of desperation on his face.

Carrie hugged Benny close. "What are you doing here?"

Behind Ross the curtain billowed in a breeze. He held one hand in the other as blood dripped between his clenched fingers.

"I'm here for you and Benny." His voice rose and fell with an odd inflection.

Tremors raced through Carrie. This couldn't be happening. They left town to be safe, so this wouldn't happen. "I'm not going with you." She inched backwards, hoping to slam the door and lock it.

As if understanding her plan, he kept pace with her.

Having tired himself out, Benny blessedly fell silent.

"You love me." Ross thrust his bloody hand toward her.

Carrie shook her head and shuffled back another step.

A stream of thick cleaning gel shot over her shoulder, hitting Ross in the neck.

"Get out of here, you hoodlum!" Thelma squeezed her

bottle again, this time aiming higher. She hit him on the cheek.

He ducked and charged Carrie.

Pain shot through her as she slammed against the wall. The force of the jolt loosened her grip on Benny. Ross worked his bloody hands between her and the baby.

One moment she held her baby, the next moment her arms were empty. She lunged at Ross, grabbing his arms and hands, trying to break his hold on the baby. "Let him go." She wanted to wrench Benny from his arms, but fear that she'd hurt Benny caused her to be careful.

Ross shook her off. With a sweep of his foot, he tripped her.

She went down hard, the shag rug burning her elbows.

Ross ran out the door holding her precious baby.

Aaron checked the back of the motel, noting the high narrow bathroom windows that could not be easily breached. There was only one door on the rear wall. He tried it and found it locked. He saw Jason dash across traffic carrying several bags and met him on the sidewalk. Relieving Jason of one bag he pointed out the rear service entrance and exit.

The hum of traffic and muted sounds of the night were shattered by a high-pitched wail.

Splinters of ice ran jagged through Aaron's veins as he and Jason sprinted for the end of the motel. It felt like forever before they reached the corner of the building and circled round to the front.

Aaron caught a glimpse of the taillights of a vehicle merging into the traffic and his heart dropped. Was that Ross leaving? The door to their room was open. Aaron charged inside, Jason on his heels.

Aaron's heart plummeted.

Carrie sat on the floor, the front of her blouse covered in blood. Thelma knelt next to her.

He tossed the bag of food on the bed and dropped to Carrie's side. "What happened?" He gently moved her hair off her shoulder, trying to find the source of the blood. She sat upright screaming. Not the actions of a person suffering from a traumatic chest wound.

She leaned against him and he hugged her, helpless to deny her what she wanted.

Incoherent, Thelma talked and cried and shook a bottle of bathroom cleanser at him.

"The window's smashed." Jason's dark voice floated to him over the surge of grief rolling off the women.

Aaron's gut twisted. "Where's Benny?" He'd never experienced anything like the terror rolling through him. His throat hurt as though he'd swallowed razors.

Jason strode into the women's room. He came back, a bleak look on his face. Squatting beside Thelma, he grasped her shoulders and gently shook her. "Tell us what happened, Thelma."

She held out the bottle of cleaner. "I sq-squirted him with this." Her hand shook.

"Who?"

"Ross." Thelma's lips trembled.

Jason's dark eyes bore into Thelma. "Did he take Benny?"

She nodded, her curls bobbing.

Carrie pressed her face to Aaron's shoulder.

He smoothed a hand over her hair. "Whose blood is this?" *Dear Lord, please don't let it be Benny's.*

"Ross's." Carrie hiccupped. "His hand was cut up."

Jason stood and walked over to the window. After a

quick inspection of the broken glass, he disappeared out the door into the early dusk.

Aaron helped Carrie stand. "Thelma, please run a face cloth under cold water for me." He helped Carrie to the bed. "Lie down." He sat beside her and bathed her face. "Tell me exactly what happened."

Her eyes were dark and glazed with fear. "He has Benny."

The torment in her words broke his heart as he struggled to give her time to tell him what happened. "What did he say?"

She shook her head. "It's my fault."

He held her hand. "You did nothing wrong."

Thelma sat on the foot of the bed holding her squeeze bottle of bathroom cleaner. "She fought him."

Aaron struggled to keep a lid on his anger.

Carrie closed her eyes. The freckles dotting her nose and cheeks stood out against the translucence of her fine skin. Her hands were cold, and he feared she might be on the verge of shock. Standing, he folded the bedspread around her.

The phone on the nightstand rang, and Aaron answered. "Black."

"Let me talk to Carrie."

The hair on the back of Aaron's neck prickled to attention. "Who is this?" He knew but wanted to keep the man talking.

"Never mind. Just let me talk to her."

Taking a deep breath, Aaron reined in his temper. "Do you have Benny?"

"He's my son." Ross's voice wavered higher, bordering on hysteria. "He's mine. And she's mine. Now let me talk to her."

Afraid he'd hang up Aaron snapped, "Hold on."

Fear swam in her eyes as he helped her sit up. He whispered in her ear. "Ross wants to talk to you. He has Benny."

She yanked the phone from his grasp, "Ross, is Benny all right?"

Aaron maneuvered to get his ear close to the receiver. Her hair tickled his cheek.

"He won't stop crying. He has to stop crying. He has to stop now."

Alarm widened Carrie's eyes. "He needs his diaper changed, Ross."

"I don't *do* that. I don't *do that*."

"I'll change him." Carrie's voice trembled. "Bring him back to me. I'll take care of him."

"No. You come to us. We're a family."

Taking her chin between his thumb and forefinger, Aaron silently moved his lips. "No."

She stared at him for only a moment before concentrating her attention on the receiver she held in her hand. "Where are you?"

Aaron scowled at her, all the time knowing he'd do the same thing.

"Where?" She bent her head and listened, pushing Aaron away when he leaned in close.

"Okay." She agreed and hung up the phone.

An ominous silence pressed in on the room. Carrie tossed aside the spread and stood. "He wants me to meet him in an old barn outside of town."

"No."

She smoothed her hair away from her face and stared at him. "He has my baby. I have no choice."

"We always have choices."

"He said I have to go alone. He specifically said he didn't want police there."

Of course he doesn't. Aaron rubbed the back of his neck.

Jason stepped into the room. Alert to the tension, he asked, "What happened?"

"Ross called." Aaron said his name with a snarl. "Wants a meeting."

Jason crossed his arms. "You call the police?"

Carrie wanted to throttle both of them. "We are *not* calling the police. He said he wanted just me or...or...." A sob broke free of the dam in her chest.

"Or what?" Aaron gently rubbed her arm, but by the look on his face he'd prefer to shake her.

"I'd never see Benny again." She paused then whispered, "Alive."

The men exchanged one of those looks that spoke volumes without either of them uttering a word.

She spoke to Thelma. "I need a bottle and formula."

"Carrie, you're not doing this." Aaron moved closer.

"I am, even if I have to walk every step of the way." Tears threatened to overwhelm Carrie. The dark looks the men directed at her fed her fear, but there was no time to indulge it. "I need diapers from the truck."

They turned their backs to her and spoke in low tones.

Thelma opened her travel purse, pulled out a tiny aerosol can, and pressed it into Carrie's hand. "Shhh."

Carrie stared at the can of pepper spray and whispered, "Thank you." She hugged Thelma and tucked the can into the diaper bag.

Thelma returned the hug before clicking her purse closed. "We're ready to go."

Jason barred the door with his tall body and crossed arms.

"What do you mean, 'we'? I don't remember inviting you to this party."

Thelma poked him in the ribs. "I'm not staying here and sitting in this room like a…like an old woman. Stop smiling. I'm still useful, you know."

With a long-suffering sigh, Jason lowered his arms and let Thelma pass.

Lines of tension bracketed Aaron's mouth.

Carrie braced herself for an argument.

His eyes narrowed. "You'll do exactly as we say."

Frustration and fear coiled deep inside her. "I can't lose Benny."

He rested the palm of his hand against her cheek, and she leaned into the warmth of his touch. "I can't lose you." He brushed her lips with the pad of his thumb.

Her heart flip-flopped, but before she could respond, he pulled away, once again all business. "Let's go." He snatched up his duffle. "You two women praying?"

This far off the main highway, there were no streetlights. The surrounding darkness pressed in on Carrie. The truck's high beams cut a narrow tunnel through the black countryside. The occasional pair of wild eyes glowed in the night making her shiver with apprehension.

The instructions were simple enough, but the road stretched on forever. She hadn't asked Ross for mileage. Afraid they were lost, she leaned between the front seats. "Are you sure this is the way?"

Aaron rode shotgun. "Have faith, Carrie."

She'd tried to pray but managed nothing more than to chant, "Please, God, help. Please, God. Please, God."

Thankfully, Thelma wasn't having the same difficulty. Since leaving their room, her eyes were closed and her lips were moving.

Fighting to keep her terror at bay, Carrie wiped her wet cheeks and sniffed. From the front seat, Aaron forced a white handkerchief into her hand. In the dim light of the dash, his eyes glimmered with moisture.

Knowing he shared her suffering gave Carrie a measure of strength. She was not alone. God was with her, and He'd sent her Aaron, Thelma, and Jason. She could do this.

"When you go in, we'll be right behind you."

She started to speak, but he held up his hand cutting her off.

"He won't know we're there. Jason has covered the truck's interior lights with duct tape. When we're closer, we'll trade places with you and Thelma. Thelma, you'll drive Carrie to the barn."

"Me?" Equal amounts of doubt and excitement threaded through the older woman's voice. "I'm gonna drive this rig?"

"Don't sound so pleased," Jason grumbled.

Thelma waved away his attitude. "My husband, Ralph, taught me to drive bigger machines than this on our farm."

Ignoring the interruption, Aaron continued to outline the plan. "Before the last leg we'll make the switch. Jason and I will climb in the back. Once we're at the barn, we'll get out when you do, Carrie. Don't slam your door. Jason will close it for you. Thelma, you're to back track until you can't see the barn. Kill the engine and lights and wait."

"Keep the doors locked," Jason added. "Don't open them for anyone but us."

Aaron looked hard at Thelma. "For your safety, I'm leaving my phone in the console."

Carrie trembled. "Is someone else out here?"
The two men exchanged "the look."
Fear zinged along every nerve in her body. "Tell me!"
They didn't say a word.

Chapter Eighteen

Carrie held Aaron's hand as he helped her into the front passenger seat. He didn't let go. Afraid to look too deeply into his eyes, she glanced at Jason helping Thelma into the driver's seat. He adjusted the seat so she could reach the pedals.

Aaron lifted Carrie's chin, urging her to look at him.

His scrutiny set her heart thundering.

"You will *not* do anything but talk to him. Understand?" His hand burrowed beneath her hair to rest on her nape. His thumb caressed beneath her ear where her pulse beat hard.

Terrified, she strained to talk around the lump in her throat. "I'll do whatever I have to do. Benny is my son."

"Leave the physical stuff to us."

"I may go with Ross."

"No." Aaron glared at her. "You'll go nowhere with that mad man."

"But if that's the only way to keep Benny alive—"

Aaron placed his thumb on her lips and shook his head. "If one of us yells for you to drop, you hit the ground immediately."

"But, why—"

"They have guns." Thelma bounced on her seat next to Carrie.

Carrie's mouth went dry. She stared at Aaron.

His eyes narrowed. "You were the one who didn't want to call in the police, remember?" He ran a hand over his hair, impatience making his voice harsh. "We have no choice." He cupped her cheeks in his hands, his look determined. "Just pray this goes well." He pressed a hard, brief kiss to her lips. With one last look into her eyes, he joined Jason in the back seat and silently closed the door.

After a few jerks and jolts, Thelma got the feel of the brakes. She drove the remaining mile to the end where the laneway widened and the barn loomed a dark silhouette. The truck's headlights bounced over dark shapes of discarded machinery crouching among scrubby bushes.

"Pull over to the right and cut the lights." Jason's spoke in a rough whisper. "Leave the engine running."

Thelma patted Carrie's hand. "Be safe, sweetie." She glanced into the rearview mirror and addressed the two men huddled behind her. "You, too."

Carrie wiped her sweaty palms on the legs of her pants and gripped the door handle. Her heart boomed in her ears, and she almost missed Aaron's low whisper to move. Swinging the door open, she slid to the ground and stepped away from the open door. *Help us, God.*

The old barn listed to the side on a stone foundation. A stiff wind would reduce the building to a dusty pile of tinder.

Out of the truck Aaron caught Carrie's elbow. He wanted to tell her not to do this. That he couldn't lose her now that he'd just found her. He didn't say either of those things. Instead, he said, "I love you." His heart pounding painfully against his ribs, he ignored her shocked expression and gently pushed her toward the yawning door and the black interior of the barn. "Go." The sooner they got this done, the happier he'd be.

Slipping into the bushes, he and Jason moved silently along the fringe of growth that rimmed the old farmyard.

Inside the barn, Carrie called out to Ross. Her voice brought an instant response from Benny.

Ross answered, his voice agitated and indistinct.

A match rasped and the glow of a flame pierced the darkness.

Aaron and Jason advanced. Benny's crying covered any noise as they positioned themselves either side of the door.

Jason signaled he was going in.

Aaron nodded. He'd wait two minutes then follow.

"Let me change him and feed him, Ross."

Carrie's plea turned Aaron's heart inside out. His nightmare had come to life.

Outside, around the corner of the barn, something rustled in the bushes.

Uneasy, Aaron dropped to a crouch, ready to pull his weapon from his ankle holster. He waited and listened, hearing nothing but the night insects buzzing and droning.

Time to go in.

Pieces of farm machinery crowded the barn floor. Aaron ducked between a harrow and a huge rake. The loose hay littering the floor silenced his footsteps. He sidled past a pile of ancient fuel cans thrown in the corner. A sharp whiff of gasoline caused the hair on the back of his neck to prickle in warning, but he kept moving closer to the center of the barn, and the lantern's circle of light.

To the left, against the wall, a rough set of stairs rose to the loft. Hay poked through the floorboards overhead. Knowing Jason would take the high ground if he saw an advantage, Aaron paused to scan the wide boards overhead. He didn't see any openings to provide a clear line of site. Jason was on ground level.

"Ross, please, he's unhappy because he needs his diaper changed." Carrie hated to beg, but she would if it meant getting her hands on her baby. Dropping the diaper bag to the floor, she stepped forward into the glow of the lantern balanced atop the wheel of an old tractor.

The polished businessman no longer existed. Blood from Ross's injured hand smeared the front of his shirt and pants. Messy and unkempt, he held Benny at arms length. "He's mine. Your mine."

Never. She swallowed back the burning bile rising in her throat. "Yes, Benny is your son. You can make him happy by letting me change him."

In the light of the kerosene lantern, Ross paced. "You're mine. You didn't say it." His eyes held a feral gleam. "Say it."

A hot tear slipped down Carrie's cheek. Aaron's "I love you" echoed in her mind. "I'm yours, too, Ross." Only fear for Benny could drag such a hideous lie from her tight throat.

Ross stopped pacing. His face contorted, and his eyes glittered with a manic light. "You're saying that so you can hold Benny." He held the whimpering baby over his head.

Frantic, Carrie shook her head as she held her hands out, wanting to touch Benny. "No. That's not true." Her heart twisted. She'd done all she could to keep her baby safe, and yet this was where she'd ended up.

"Then why's your guard dog still hanging around? Where is he?" Ross peered around, holding Benny high.

Panic seized Carrie. "The truck left."

"Where is he?" The pitch of his voice grew hysterical. His breath came in short bursts and his gaze darted about the barn's dim interior as though trying to see into the shadows. He glanced overhead beyond the baby he held. "No stone angel eyes watching me. Not here in a barn. Not here." He shuddered.

Carrie stepped closer. "It's okay. I'm here. With you." Her heart rebelled, but she refused to back away.

His lips were contorted in a diabolical snarl. "Say you love me."

Carrie inched closer.

Ross lifted Benny high, out of her reach and screamed, "Say it!"

Barely able to speak beyond the terror lodged in her throat, her voice croaked. "I love you." Aaron's dear face flashed through her mind. Her breath caught in her throat.

"He stinks." Ross lowered Benny, holding him away from his body.

"Let me help." Her fingertips grazed Benny's fat thigh clothed in wet dungarees.

The moment Ross released Benny to Carrie he grabbed a fistful of her hair and pulled.

She squealed as pain radiated across her scalp and down her neck.

He twisted his fingers deeper in the red-gold strands. "I always liked your hair." With her hair stretched taut between them, he controlled her. He pulled her to where the diaper bag lay on the floor.

A quick yank brought fresh tears to her eyes. "Please let go, Ross."

"No."

Ignoring the pain, she cuddled Benny close as she knelt beside the diaper bag. *God, where are you?* Pulling a baby blanket from the bag, she spread it on the musty hay and placed Benny on his back. She fought the urge to search the dark corners of the barn for Aaron and Jason.

"Hurry up." Ross gave her hair another cruel twist.

Focused on Benny, she breathlessly hummed a mindless tune to soothe him as she went through the motions of removing his wet diaper and cleaning him up. Reaching into her bag for ointment, her fingers brushed the cool aerosol can of pepper spray. Her breathing escalated. Did she dare? Hands trembling, she changed Benny and stuffed the ointment into the diaper bag.

Time stood still. Her hand in the bag, she uncapped the spray and positioned her finger.

"What are you doing?" Ross leaned close to see.

In one quick motion, Carrie pulled out the can and sprayed him in the face.

His shriek released the terror building inside her. Shaking, she dropped the can and snatched Benny up. A shadow to her right moved. Aaron stood at her side and pulled her to her feet.

Ross staggered and clawed blindly at his eyes, screaming and cursing. He bumped the lantern with his elbow just as Jason loomed behind him. The lantern fell to the floor. Kerosene hissed, and fire bloomed in the hay under foot.

Aaron grabbed Carrie's arm and hauled her away from the fire and the struggling men. In his chest his heart swelled with fear. He glanced over his shoulder. Ash and cinders burned hot on his skin as flames raced up the wooden support beams silhouetting Jason and Ross in a life and death struggle.

Curled protectively over Benny, Carrie followed his lead. The roar of the flames beat at his ears, and the heat scorched his back. Acrid smoke robbed him of his breath.

Would God spare Carrie and Benny only to take Jason's life?

If ever he needed a miracle, now was the time. Aaron blinked away the smoke induced tears distorting his vision. Counting three men, he shook his head and blinked hard.

A bright flash lit up the barn's interior. A deafening explosion followed.

Aaron's nightmare and reality jumbled together in the chaos of the moment. Tightening his arm around Carrie, he plunged through the open door. She fell to her knees. "Don't stop. Keep going." He pulled her up and lurched for the edge of the yard, but she stumbled and fell again.

"Come on, Carrie." Aaron pulled on her arm. He looked back, desperate to see Jason come out the door. Barn timbers cracked and fell, scattering hot glowing embers into the night. The heat of the fire pushed against them like an unseen wall. The hot air scorched the lining of his throat.

The silhouette of two men emerged from the inferno. They staggered and stumbled through the high weeds to the side of the barn before falling to the ground.

"Stay here." Aaron settled Carrie and Benny on a pile of rocks from a tumbled down stone wall. "Don't move."

In the bright light of the blaze, one man got up. Too short to be Jason, Aaron rushed him. The guy yelped in surprise before they hit the ground. Breathing smoke-filled air, Aaron rolled his opponent and raised his fist.

Not Ross, but he looked familiar. Aaron clutched the man's singed shirt and shook him. "Who are you?"

Wheezing and struggling to breathe, the man beneath Aaron raised his burned and blistered hands in surrender. He coughed. "See to your friend."

Hesitating only a moment, Aaron leapt off the man and fell to his knees beside Jason. At the sight of his partner, his heart slowed to a heavy drumbeat. "Dear Lord." The sickening smell of burned flesh and clothing turned Aaron's stomach.

The man he'd almost punched leaned over and grasped Jason's feet. "Let's move him away from the building."

Aaron lifted Jason under his shoulders. They moved him to a patch of soft moss away from the burning barn.

"Jase." His throat raw from smoke and grief, Aaron struggled to talk. A heavy hand rested on his shoulder.

"Hey, buddy. We're here to help now." An older man in a fire helmet emblazoned with CHIEF knelt beside Jason and checked for a pulse. He motioned for the men getting out of a van marked RESCUE.

Volunteer firefighters were arriving in pickups and family cars. Hauling turnout gear from backseats and trunks, they suited up. Over the crackling roar of the fire, sirens screamed and lights flashed as the fire trucks arrived.

Aaron spoke to the chief. "There's another man inside."

The chief studied the fully involved structure and shook his head. "I'm sorry. The barn is too far gone to go in."

Knowing he was in the way, Aaron cast one last look at his friend and backed away. Giving a wide berth to the men laying hose from the tanker truck, he walked to the wall where he'd left Carrie.

Thelma had joined her. She addressed Aaron. "I called 911 as soon as I saw the flames."

"Thank you." He squatted in front of Carrie. The look in her eyes when she pulled her gaze away from the burning barn would forever be etched in his memory.

"How are Ross and Jason?" The shrill peal of sirens and the crackling roar of the fire almost drowned out her voice.

He stroked her cheek. "The rescue team is working on Jason," he paused, "and another man."

Against the backdrop of yellow and orange flames, the firemen were dark silhouettes.

"Not Ross?" she asked.

"No."

Her chest rose and fell as she struggled to maintain control of her emotions. "I don't want him dead." She held Benny closer.

Aaron smoothed hair from her face. "This is not your fault, Carrie. Ross knocked over the lantern."

"Is Jason...?" Her voice broke.

"He's alive." He didn't know anything more than that. For the moment that was enough.

A noisy ruckus burst out where the emergency medical techs worked on Jason and the other man.

Someone broke free from the group. The man Aaron pulled off Jason stumbled toward him, an EMT on either side supporting him.

Carrie gasped. *"Him!"* She handed Benny to Thelma and rose to her feet.

Aaron stood next to her, steadying her with an arm around her shoulders. "You recognize him?"

"He's the man from the mall." A tremor ran through her. "The man that tipped over the clothes rack and spilled the drink on Ross."

Sweeping her behind him, Aaron placed himself between Carrie and the man.

Burt tried to shake off his escorts, but they stuck like chewing gum on the sole of his shoe. His hands throbbed beneath a layer of gauze. His face pained him. Even his hair hurt. They were insisting he go to the hospital. He'd go, but in his own time. Unsteady, he plowed on noting the sheriff's arrival. *Marvelous. Let's make it a party.*

He stopped in front of biker boy. He'd never learned the guy's name. "I want to talk to Carrie Lillibridge."

"What's she to you?"

Burt sighed. "Just doing my job." *Wrong thing to say.* "Let go of me. Your partner would still be in that inferno if I hadn't pulled half the barn off him and hauled him out."

"Anything you want to say to her, you can say to me."

Burt stared at the young man, wishing he could remember being that young and full of vinegar.

"Aaron, let's hear what he has to say." Carrie moved to stand beside the biker.

"Thank you." Burt tried to stand straighter but gave up when pain coursed through him. He leaned heavily against the man on his right. "My name is Burt Campbell, Ms. Lillibridge. You sure have an entertaining life. It's about to become more interesting."

The biker, who now had a name—Aaron—gave him a hard look. "You were the man in the sedan?"

"Yeah." Burt shrugged and winced. Didn't take biker boy, *Aaron*, long to put the pieces together.

Aaron's eyes narrowed. "Why did you try to break into Carrie's apartment?"

Carrie gasped and stared at Burt.

Burt snorted. *As if.* "I was only looking around."

"Why?"

He liked this part of a case best. Everyone reacted differently. Ignoring Aaron, Burt concentrated on Carrie.

"I work for someone, and she wants to meet you."

Confusion flitted across the young lady's face.

Her protector-in-chief got all growly. "Who do you work for?"

Burt had to get this done before he collapsed into the arms of the EMTs. "Vanessa Rochelle."

Carrie gasped. "The designer?"

Burt nodded. "Your mother."

Chapter Nineteen

Aaron raced along the hospital's gleaming corridor. The five hours at the sheriff's office were the longest hours of his life. He could still feel the weight of Carrie's unconscious body in his arms. Upon hearing Burt's surprising news, she'd fainted. Thankfully, Thelma had been holding the baby. He rounded a corner and bumped into Thelma, catching her before she toppled over.

Lines of exhaustion were etched in her pale face. She'd bundled Benny in one of Carrie's sweaters. Leading her to a chair tucked into a small alcove, he helped her sit. "Are you and Benny okay?"

She nodded, shifting the sleeping infant into a more comfortable position. "Exhausted."

He needed to find a place for her and Benny to stay for what was left of the night. "Where's Carrie?"

Thelma nodded toward a room across the hall. "They wanted to keep her for observation."

He patted her hand. "Wait here for me."

His heart in his throat, he entered Carrie's hospital room. Her long lashes lay in a fiery crescent on each cheek. Her hair blazed bright against the white bed linens. He stroked her hand with his fingers, proving to himself she was alive.

A tiny frown squeezed her brow, and her eyes fluttered open.

"Hi." Aaron leaned closer. "How're you feeling?"

She yawned wide and indelicately. Totally Carrie. "They drug me?"

He grinned. "Probably." He held her hand in his.

The mist cleared in her beautiful green eyes, replaced by a sharp pained look. "Ross is dead, isn't he?"

Aaron didn't want to talk about Ross. He wanted to talk about their future together, but she needed to lay her ghosts to rest so he nodded. "Yeah." He didn't know how to comfort her. Was she relieved the creep wouldn't bother her again? Or would she feel guilty, believing his death was her fault.

"I've just spent hours with the sheriff. They'll want to talk to you, too."

"Okay." Her eyes glistened with unshed tears.

He kissed her forehead, her skin warm and silky against his lips. Patience wasn't one of his virtues. For so long he'd vowed he wouldn't have a family. But after the last forty-eight hours, he was prepared to risk everything to keep this woman and her baby by his side. His heart double-timed in his chest. "I meant what I said, you know."

She frowned again. "What?"

"I love you." His voice cracked and his ears burned.

Her eyes grew wide, so he rushed on. "I never allowed myself to dream of having a family. My job is risky, and you know babies scared the bejabbers out of me." He shook his head. "Until I met you and Benny. Somehow your little boy managed to weasel his way past my fears and wrap himself around my heart."

She looked so small and pale lying in the hospital bed.

He leaned closer. "So did his mother." Taking a deep breath, he finished the dive into unknown waters. "If you're willing, I'd like to make a go at having a family, Carrie, with you and Benny." *Way to be eloquent, Black.*

She didn't say anything and unease curled through his stomach. Quiet was not a word he'd ever use to describe Carrie. Was he making a fool of himself? Maybe she loved someone else. She'd said as much when she got the flowers on her doorstep. Never seeing another man around, he'd dismissed the idea.

She licked her lips. "Are you asking me to marry you?"

He expelled the breath he'd been holding in one big huff. "Yeah. I am. Will you marry me, Carrie Lillibridge?"

She turned her head away. "I'm sorry. No. I can't."

Wrong answer. Pain speared through him. His grip on the bed rail tightened. His knuckles turned white. "Who are you seeing? Where is he?" Not wanting to believe the blank look in her eyes, he leaned over the bed. "The flower guy. Remember him?"

Her cheeks blazed pink. "I made him up."

Before he could respond, she grabbed his wrist. "Ross said he'd hurt you. I wanted you to go away so he wouldn't hurt you."

"*You* were protecting *me*?" He gripped the bed rail in frustration. "What if I *had* minded my own business?" He shuddered.

She scowled at him, gunning for a fight. Nothing would be resolved tonight. As much as he hated to leave, he released his grip on the rail and backed off. "My timing is poor. Guess this isn't the time or place for a marriage proposal." Though at this point, he'd settle for a simple "I love you" real easy. He couldn't help himself. He brushed an errant wisp of hair from her cheek.

"I can't marry you." Her voice wobbled. "I have to think of Benny and what's best...." She gulped. "And my...my mother. I have no idea what that man was talking about, but I want to find out."

He backed away, trying to distance himself from the hurt, from caring, from the best thing that ever happened to him. Not wanting her to see she'd left him wounded and bleeding, he stepped to the door. "Since there's no need to continue on to Chicago, I'll take you, Benny, and Thelma home after they release you."

He fumbled the door handle and leaned against the wall outside her room, his quaking knees refusing to do their job. He pushed the pain into a tiny box in his heart and forced himself to think. She'd tried to protect him. He clung to the knowledge she felt something for him as he headed toward the burn unit to check on Jason.

Carrie crushed the crisp bed sheets in her hands. Her heart ached, and she wanted to call him back. Wanted to wrap her arms around him and hold on. At the barn, in a moment of clarity, she thought she loved Aaron. But she'd been wrong about love once before. Why did love come with so many uncertainties? She buried her face in the pillow and wept. She cried until the tears ran dry, and her throat burned raw.

The acrid scent of smoke penetrated her fog of anguish. Her heart thumped with the small hope Aaron had come back. She pushed aside her damp pillow.

The man named Burt stood at her bedside. His face looked as though he'd suffered a severe sunburn. His clothes were sooty and spotted with burn holes.

He spoke first. "I'm a private investigator working for Vanessa Rochelle."

Carrie shifted to face him. "You said she's my mother?"

He nodded. "She hired me to find you." He shifted uncomfortably. "That night at your house, I wasn't trying to break in. Several times I watched you drive like a woman possessed and run for the safety of your house." He brushed his hand across his hair and bits of ash fell to his shoulders. "Knew you were scared. Was just checking you were home safe. Wanted to see what kind of a lock you had on that backdoor."

Carrie stared at him, trying to fit the bits together. It seemed Aaron hadn't been the only one looking out for her. "Did you push the clothes rack over on purpose?"

He nodded. "Yeah."

"And the Maui Wowie?"

A hint of a smile touched his lips. "Made a mess with that, didn't I?"

Carrie smiled. "Thank you." She plucked at the sheet covering her legs. "After all this time, why is my mother looking for me now?" Long ago she'd let go of the dream of meeting her mother. "Why did she let me go in the first place?"

Burt shrugged. "You'll have to ask her." He walked to the window and looked outside. "She didn't know if you'd want to meet her after so many years."

"I'm not sure I do." Carrie crossed her arms. Fear and petulance fired through her. She couldn't expect the woman to love her. But what if her mother didn't like her or approve of her? Could she face her mother's rejection a second time?

"Give her a chance, Ms. Lillibridge. At least let her explain. After that decide if she's worthy of your love."

Stunned by his words, she could only stare at his retreating back. Vanessa Rochelle worthy of *her* love? That wasn't the question. More to the point, would Vanessa Rochelle, the toast of the fashion accessories world, think *Carrie* deserving of love?

A nurse whisked in followed by two deputies from the sheriff's department. "Are you feeling well enough to talk to these men?"

She wasn't. She'd never be ready, but she nodded. The sooner she finished the interview, the sooner she could go home. Her heart flip-flopped. Home. Would Aaron remain in his apartment upstairs?

Running on empty Aaron lugged the last of the luggage up the front porch steps. He set a suitcase in side Carrie's door. "I'll see you later."

Her wan smile made his heart squeeze. He climbed the stairs to his apartment. The ride home had been quiet. The women and Benny had slept in the truck's backseat.

His apartment hadn't changed. It was still a depressing sight. Almost everything in the place belonged to someone else. He switched on the fan—*his* fan—and flopped onto the couch to let the cool breeze sweep over him. The day he and Carrie bought the fan played through his mind. Their search for her toaster, the flying linens, and the shared laughter. And the old man assuming he and Carrie were married.

Maybe he hadn't corrected the old fellow because somewhere deep inside even then he'd hoped.... He jumped off the couch and turned off the fan. *You need a shower and sleep, Black.* He headed down the hall, peeling off his t-shirt as he went.

Thelma sat on Carrie's couch and fanned herself. "I've had enough excitement to last me the rest of my life."

Carrie smiled. "I'm looking forward to a shower."

"With lots of shampoo." Thelma ran a wrinkled hand through her flattened curls. "I didn't have the strength to do it last night in the hotel."

Placing the baby in the playpen, Carrie sprawled next to her dear friend. "Keep praying for me, Auntie."

Thelma squeezed her hand. "I am, sweetie. But remember, Ross made his choices."

Carrie leaned her head back. "In the barn...." Her voice caught, and she cleared her throat. "At the end he sounded unbalanced and sick." A tear trailed down her cheek. "What will I tell Benny when he's old enough to ask about his father?"

Thelma *pat-patted* her hand. "When the time comes, you'll know what to say. God will show you. Now tell me about that man, Burt Campbell. Your mother employed him?"

Carrie sat up. "That's what he said. What I can't figure out is why this sudden interest in me. I mean, *years* have passed since she left me in state care and never looked back."

"Ask her."

"I will if I choose to see her. I'm not so sure I want to." Carrie ignored the little girl crying inside. An adult with a son of her own, her job was to give him a secure future. What if Benny got to know his grandmother and love her? If Vanessa lost interest in them could she survive losing her mother all over again?

Carrie reached for Thelma. Wrapped in her trusted friend's arms, she wept.

Chapter Twenty

Carrie stacked diapers in a cubby beneath the changing table and put away the rompers she'd packed for the trip to Chicago. She leaned over the crib and watched Benny sleep. With so much to be thankful for she still felt the heavy weight of sadness press in on her. She wiped her eyes with a tissue. Playing a part in Ross's horrible death haunted her. His screams still echoed in her mind.

Tossing the tissue in the wastebasket, she walked into the living room and moved the last of the empty totes and luggage into the hall closet.

Booted feet thundered on the stairs, rattling the ceramic flamingos on the shelf by the door. She listened to Aaron leave the house. The normalcy of the moment shook her. Life went on. Hurrying to the window, she peeked out.

Dressed in the usual black t-shirt and jeans, Aaron strapped a lumpy duffle behind his seat.

Her heart bumped hard. Was he leaving without saying goodbye? She hadn't seen him since yesterday afternoon when he'd brought in the last of the luggage. She let the curtain drop into place and listened to his bike roar out onto the street. What if she never saw him again? The ache around her heart grew larger.

Needing the warm comfort of a cup of tea, she put the kettle of water on to boil and set out a cup and saucer. Ross was gone. Because of the circumstances surrounding his death she hadn't expected to feel happy. She'd hoped for a sense of relief. But her conversation with Burt and Aaron's proposal had left her unsettled.

As Carrie sipped her second cup of tea, someone knocked on her apartment door. Her heart gave a tiny leap. Had Aaron come back? She hadn't heard his bike. She hurried to her door.

A woman with hair the same color as hers stood in the foyer. She was dressed in a tailored navy suit and elegant high heels.

Carrie stood in stunned silence, recognizing the woman from the pages of fashion magazines. Her breath lodged in her throat.

"Carrie Lillibridge?" The woman's voice was smooth and breathless.

Unable to speak, Carrie nodded.

"I'm Vanessa Rochelle." She held out a manicured hand. "I'm your mother."

So many times as a child, Carrie had dreamed of this moment and the happiness of a reunion. Now that the day was finally here, terror swamped her. What if they didn't like each other? The hope of "some day" would be gone.

Carrie stood frozen in place. She should ask this woman—her mother—to come in, but the simple words couldn't get past the fear lodged in her throat, so she extended her trembling hand.

The woman smiled and grasped it in both of hers. Her gaze shifted past Carrie to take in the living room.

Carrie pulled her hand away and stepped aside. Her mother entered and stood in the middle of the rug, gazing at the painting that hung over the couch.

Heart racing, Carrie tried to look at her home through the eyes of a stranger. She loved the vibrant colors of the bullfighter. The doilies dotting the room and each flamingo in her collection had a story. The value of each item came from having a place in the new life she'd built for herself and Benny. Would Vanessa understand that or look down her nose at Carrie and her simple life.

Panic began to build inside her. She had so many questions, but fear silenced her.

Aaron turned his bike onto Margin Street. Before taking off to run errands, which included a trip to the laundromat, he'd called the hospital to check on Jason. The doctor was pleased with the way Jason was responding to care, but it would be some time before he could leave the hospital. When he did, he'd have decisions to make if his injuries prevented him from going back to his old job.

After speaking with the doctor, Aaron had called Chicago and filled in the chief. He no longer felt the eagerness to get back into the fray. And other than his job, his days and nights in the city were empty. Perhaps he could convince Jason to build a life here in this small seacoast town.

His thoughts shifted to Carrie and his heart gave a funny little zing. Could he convince her he was serious about marriage? Trying to come up with a plan had kept him awake most of the night.

A red sports car was parked behind Carrie's wagon. Pulling into the driveway, he stared at the out-of-state plates.

Her mother. Her *wealthy* mother. Carrie wouldn't have any need for a washed-up cop hanging around if what Burt said was true. He grabbed his duffle, now filled with clean clothes, and climbed the front steps. He'd just go on upstairs and spend the next few hours pacing, wishing he were a flamingo on the shelf in Carrie's apartment.

He stepped through the front foyer door.

Carrie stood framed in her open apartment door. Her eyes had that deer-in-the-headlights look.

Aaron's heart stuttered. He tossed his duffel on the stairs and approached her. "You okay?"

She didn't answer.

He glanced past her. A woman stood in the center of the living room. Her mother. No one else would have the same red-gold hair and green eyes.

He ushered her into the apartment and closed the door. Extending his hand he introduced himself. "Aaron Black."

"Vanessa Rochelle."

Tension filled the room as the two women kept glancing at each other, but neither one attempted to start a conversation.

Aaron gestured toward the couch. "Have a seat, ladies."

They carefully sat at either end on the edge of the cushions, ready to pop up and run at the slightest provocation.

He shook his head. "I don't know what's supposed to happen when," he looked pointedly at Carrie, "you meet a long lost mother." He frowned at her mother. "Or daughter. But seems to me, the only way the two of you can figure out where you stand with each other is to talk."

A quiet rustle came from Benny's bedroom.

Nice predicament you've led me into, Lord. Got any ideas on how I should proceed? If you're handing out miracles today, now is a good time to send one to Margin Street.

Hoping to get to Benny before he started to cry, Aaron looked at the women staring back at him with identical looks of panic. "Yeah. Okay. Hold that thought." He bolted for Benny's room. "Hey, kiddo." He lifted the baby and cradled him close as he walked back down the hall.

Benny squirmed and Aaron shifted him to the crook of his arm as he entered the living room. "Hang on, little fella. We're handling a crisis between your mother and your grandma."

The two women gasped.

A sensation of warmth brushed through Aaron, and he knew what he had to do. The answer to his prayer was a doozy. *Thank you, Father.*

He stepped in front of Carrie's mother. "Meet your grandson, Benjamin Lillibridge." Without missing a beat, he plunked the baby on Vanessa Rochelle's silk clad lap.

The woman instinctively lifted her bejeweled hands to hold the baby. For a long moment, Benny and she just looked into each other's eyes. The baby patted her face with a chubby hand.

A tear rolled down her cheek, followed by another and then another. Her face contorted and she pulled him close to muffle a sob against Benny's plump neck. She cried with noisy abandon.

Just like her daughter. Aaron rubbed a hand over the back of his neck as he watched the two women.

Carrie was crying along with her mother. Longing, anxiety, and a hundred other emotions flitted across her beautiful face.

Aaron grasped her hand and tugged, forcing her to move closer to her mother. He'd done all he could do. It was up to Carrie now. Hopefully, she'd draw on her faith and courage just as she had when fighting to protect Benny.

Their anguish caused his heart to ache. Though their tears made him uncomfortable he couldn't leave. He hovered protectively, his feet rooted to the floor.

Carrie rubbed at her cheeks. Her mother held Benny and cried like a banshee. She wanted to cry and laugh and hug her and tell her to leave all at the same time. Confusion reigned supreme, so she did what she always did at times like this. She prayed. *Father, help me. Help me do what Jesus would do.*

The fog cleared so swiftly, Carrie felt light-headed. She forced a shaky breath around the aching lump at the base of her throat and touched her mother's shoulder. The earth moved on its axis. Her fingers played over the nubby fabric of the suit and stroked a silky strand of hair.

All her life she'd tried to remember her mother. Even when angry with the woman who'd given her up, a corner of her heart longed to know her. That woman now sat on Carrie's couch, holding Benny and weeping.

A box of tissues landed on Carrie's lap. Giving Aaron a watery smile of thanks, she used one to wipe her eyes and blow her nose. She nudged her mother's arm and held out a tissue for her. Taking Benny, she gave her mother time to pull herself together.

"Why are you here now?" Carrie couldn't hold back the question any longer.

Vanessa tugged at the hem of her skirt. "I've wanted to find you for ages." Her voice trembled. "But I was afraid. If I found you, I didn't know if I could face you. I wondered if you would hate me."

The lump in Carrie's throat grew bigger.

Her mother twisted the tissue she held. "But not knowing was killing me. What did you look like? Were you married? Did you have children? I finally hired Burt. He's a good man. He found out so much for me." Her gaze flicked to Benny then back to her hands in her lap. "But he kept some secrets, too." Vanessa's voice became soft. "He didn't tell me I had a grandson."

Carrie's voice was a raw whisper. "Why did you send me into foster care? Why...?" Her voice failed her, and fat tears rolled down her cheeks. The couch dipped beside her, and Aaron's arm wrapped protectively across her back.

Taking courage from his presence she blinked away her tears and looked at her mother. She wanted to see her mother's face when she heard for the first time why she'd become a ward of the state.

Vanessa snatched another tissue from the box. "Your father—" Her voice caught.

A jolt rocked through Carrie. *Her father.* She'd speculated about him, on occasion. But it was her mother she thought about most as a child.

Her mother sniffed. "Your father was a wonderful young man. I loved him. We wanted to marry. Poor as church mice, but we had big dreams." She shook her head. "The marriage wasn't meant to be. One foggy night he was killed in an accident on the highway. Soon after his funeral, I discovered I was pregnant with you."

A chill ran through Carrie. She leaned against Aaron, trying to absorb his warmth. She jumped when her mother touched her knee.

"You were a beautiful baby. My parents—they tried to help me. We—you and I—lived with them, but they were only just getting by, too." She wiped away a tear. "I was so young...and angry because I'd lost Jonathan. My heart ached for him. Soon after his death I discovered alcohol. The hurt dulled for a few hours when I drank. My parents babysat you when I went out with friends and partied until dawn."

Aaron ran his hand across Carrie's back. His voice held a hard note. "Did you mistreat Carrie?"

Vanessa looked at him with shock. "No. Oh dear, no. But, eventually, I just…never came home. My parents were your sole caregivers." She gulped. "My mother, your grandmother, passed away. My father was unwell. He couldn't care for an infant. And even if he had known where to find me, I was too irresponsible to care for you. He did the only thing he could do. He placed you in state foster care. It broke his heart. He died soon after that."

Sheltered in the crook of Aaron's arm, Carrie sifted through the information, overwhelmed by all she'd learned. Her grandparents had loved her. And her mother was here…. She licked her dry lips and whispered, "I've always wondered."

Vanessa patted her eyes with the tissue. "I'm so sorry. I regret what I did…leaving you like that. Please believe me when I say, I never regretted having you." She patted Benny's leg. "Your son is beautiful." A smile curved her lips. "If you can bring yourself to forgive me, I'd like to get to know you and your little boy."

Carrie could barely take a breath. Aaron's arm tightened around her. Her mother's honesty surprised her. If she wanted this relationship to work, she'd have to offer the same. "I've been angry for years…."

"I'm so sorry," Vanessa whispered.

Her words were a balm to Carrie's aching heart. She bit her bottom lip. Vanessa had searched for Carrie, longing for forgiveness. *Like when you found Jesus.* The gentle whisper echoed through Carrie's mind and tears sprang into her eyes.

Did her mother know Jesus? Would forgiving Vanessa bring her mother one step closer to seeking out God's love and forgiveness? Carrie's heart raced. Could she let go of the anger? It had been a part of her for so long.

The warmth of God's presence feathered through her followed by that still small voice she couldn't ignore.

Release the anger.

Trembling, Carrie handed Benny to Aaron. His smile was tender and filled with reassurance. His confidence in her gave her the courage she needed. She faced her mother. "I'd like to know more about you, too." Just saying the words untied a knot deep inside Carrie. Healing took time. They had years to make up for. Today was a beginning.

She reached for her mother. Silky hair like her own caressed her cheek. Expensive perfume tickled her nose. Wrapped in her mother's arms filled with love felt good...and right...and maybe a little like heaven.

The couch cushion twanged as Aaron rose. "Well, Benny my boy, guess we'll leave the women to their weeping. We've got things to do." He snagged the extra diaper bag hanging on the coat tree and headed for the door. He winked at Carrie and was gone.

Her mother pulled away and looked at her with eyes so much like her own. "He seems like a nice man. Is he Benny's father?"

Taking a deep breath, Carrie sent a prayer winging heavenward. *Help me be honest.* "Mother, you're not the only one who's made poor choices." She looked at their entwined hands resting on her mother's knee. "Would you like a cup of tea?"

Chapter Twenty-one

Aaron walked up the stairs to his apartment two at a time, gently bouncing a giggling Benny with each step. He was proud of Carrie. She had courage. Hopefully, she didn't have any other demons to face because he wasn't sure his heart would survive.

He left his apartment door open, wanting to hear Vanessa leave. Dropping the diaper bag on the floor he sat on the couch and scooted into a slouched position so he could rest his feet on the edge of the coffee table. He raised his knees high and braced Benny's back against his thighs so they were face to face.

"So, kiddo, what do you think about that? You got yourself a granny today." His big hands closed gently around Benny's fat sides. "She looks just like your mama. Peas in a pod. Life's gonna be downright interesting from now on."

Not that life had been mundane before today. But now the peril had changed. The physical danger was gone in exchange for hazards of the heart. Not exactly his area of expertise.

"We need a plan." He wiped the drool off Benny's chin

with the pad of his thumb. "We have to convince your mama we're a team. You, and me, and her."

The hem of Benny's blue and white striped shirt crept up, revealing a round Buddha belly. Unable to resist, Aaron lifted Benny high and blew a sloppy raspberry against the sweetly scented skin.

Benny giggled, and Aaron's heart flipped. Hopefully the little guy wouldn't need a diaper change on his watch. He'd made mental notes about the process, but the "ew" factor climbed too high on occasion. Up to now he'd avoided the task at all cost.

Aaron swung the diaper bag onto the couch. "Got anything fun in here?"

Benny smiled and waved his arms with abandon.

In a small pocket on the front of the bag, Aaron found a pacifier. "Want this?" He slipped the nipple between Benny's lips.

Benny promptly spit it out.

"Okay. That's a no." Aaron dug into the next pocket. "How about this?" He held up a colorful rattle and gave it a shake.

Benny grabbed it from him and promptly threw the toy, hitting Aaron squarely on the brow.

"Yo, buddy. Cool left hook you got there." Aaron continued to paw through the bag. Soon diapers, ointment, bibs, a romper, a can of formula, and a clean bottle littered the couch.

Putting his fingers in a small inside pocket, he dug out three ponytail holders. "Whoa, buddy. Major find." He sat Benny securely at the base of his thighs. "See these?" He held them up. "Your mother has a habit of losing them. I'm obsessed with finding them." He twisted a dark blue one shot through with sparkly threads around his forefinger. "You could say I'm a collector." He entwined the orange one around his little finger. "Problem is, if your mom doesn't see me as part of the team, my source of ponytail holders dries up." The thought put a damper on his mood.

Slipping one end of stretchy tie-dyed fabric around his ring finger, he twisted it and slipped the other end over his middle finger. "'Course, I could buy them in the store, but that isn't the same." He stared at his hand for a long moment. "Not by a long shot."

Benny gurgled and kicked Aaron in the stomach.

"What if I told your mama she doesn't have to marry me? Just let me hang around to pick up her ponytail holders."

Benny stuck out his tongue and blew sloppy bubbles.

"Yeah. I didn't think so either." Grabbing a bib, he wiped Benny's wet chin. "So, you have a better plan?" He held his hand in front of the baby and let him swat at the colorful fabric. Curious to know how things were going one floor below, he fought the temptation to take Benny outside and stand under an open window. "Not a good idea, Black," he muttered. "It's none of your business. Let them sort things out on their own." Would Carrie leave to live with her mother? His heart hurt just thinking about the possibility. "How about we pray about this, kiddo?"

The baby smiled and Aaron smiled back. "Good. I'll start." Lifting Benny, he placed him on his chest and rested his chin on the top of the baby's fuzzy head. A soft wisp of hair tickled him, and he blinked hard. He was going soft and enjoying every minute of it.

Closing his eyes, he sighed. "Lord, Benny and I want to talk to You. First of all, be with Carrie and Vanessa downstairs as they figure things out. Give Benny the chance to know his grandmother. A boy needs a grandmother." His thoughts drifted to his own grandmother. He'd been in his share of trouble as a kid, but he'd always known she loved him unconditionally.

Pulling his thoughts back on track, he continued. "Where was I? Oh, yeah. Help Carrie to see that we'd be great as a family. A boy needs a daddy, too." Eyes still closed he kissed the top of Benny's head.

"If we're together, I can teach him to play baseball and catch fireflies. I'd be sure he grows up knowing You and honoring his mother. And about his mother—help me show Carrie how much I love her. Let her come to love me, too. She has a lot to think about right now with finding her mom and Ross's death. I want to help her." He sighed deeply, praying from his heart. "I want to love her and have that love returned."

A floorboard creaked.

Aaron opened his eyes and looked straight into luminous green eyes.

"Carrie!" Lifting Benny, he stood, feeling lost and a little foolish. How much did she hear? He couldn't tell. Her tears may be from the visit with her mother.

"Hi." Her voice was a whisper.

"Hi, yourself." He switched Benny to his other shoulder. "Did your visit go okay with your mom?"

She nodded. Her glance ricocheted between the jumble of baby things on his couch and him.

Heat flashed across his face. "We were playing."

Carrie clung to the doorframe hoping her legs didn't let her down. Hearing Aaron pray created a rush of longing so strong, she could barely breathe. She didn't trust her judgment when it came to men. Did she have the courage to trust God and His plan? Was her faith strong enough?

She stepped into the room and stopped in front of Aaron. His big hand patted and soothed Benny, who was all drooly and drowsy with contentment. She plucked at the ponytail holders wrapped around Aaron's fingers. "See you found these."

He looked at her sheepishly and shrugged. "Yeah. I collect them."

"You should have something other than a boot to keep them in."

"How'd you—"

She giggled. "I looked in your duffle the night of…the night—" She gulped and hurried over to the couch. Sweeping aside the baby things, she took Benny from Aaron and settled him on the cushions, wedging a pillow in front of him for safety. When she looked at Aaron, his arms were crossed and legs braced.

"So you rifled through my duffle."

"Only your boot."

"I find them everywhere."

"Were you planning on giving them back?"

A ghost of a grin played across his lips as he stepped closer. "Actually, I planned on holding them hostage till you agreed to go on a date with me."

A date? She should close her mouth, but…he wanted to go on a *date*? After all they'd experienced, he wanted to go on a *date*. Like they were strangers and didn't know each other.

The thought rocked her. She knew him. Really *knew* him. Aaron was loyal and rock steady. He risked his life for her and Benny. He never ridiculed her or did anything to make her distrust him. She stepped closer to him.

He uncrossed his arms and looked at her askance. "What?" His voice rasped with uncertainty.

"I don't want to go on a date."

His Adam's apple bobbed. "I just figured if we started over again...."

She placed her hands on either side of his face. "I don't want to start over again." A hot tear trailed down her cheek.

"You don't?" His eyes were filled with doubt.

"Nope." Running the pad of her thumb across his cheek, she asked, "Did you mean it?"

"What?" His voice was sandpaper rough.

"You'd teach Benny how to catch fireflies?"

His breath hitched, and he nodded.

"And play baseball?"

"Yes."

She slipped her hands to his shoulders. "And honor his mother?"

"Oh, yeah." His mouth cracked into a small smile as though he knew where this conversation was going.

"I still don't want a date." She tried to scowl at him and confusion flashed across his dear face. She needed to put both of them out of their misery. "But I would like a wedding."

His mouth fell open.

For a moment, time stood still. But only for a moment.

He swept her into his arms and swung her in a circle.

"Aaron!"

His joyful whoop rang in her ears. Her feet hit the floor, and she grabbed his arms to stave off the vertigo threatening to buckle her knees.

His kiss was everything she dreamed a kiss should be—warm and tender and oh, so right.

He backed off and held her at arms length. "Are you sure?"

Between the laughter and the tears, she managed to squeak, "Yes."

"What changed your mind?" Happiness gleamed in the dark depths of his eyes.

"I didn't change my mind. I just haven't had the courage to believe this is real." Clinging to his hand she followed him to the couch.

He sat and pulled her onto his knee.

Her heart fluttered beneath his warm gaze.

Sweeping a strand of hair from her face, he said, "In the barn, when you told Ross you loved him—"

"That was a lie."

He hugged her close. "I hated hearing you say that to him, but I didn't believe for a minute you meant it."

She draped her arm across his shoulders and kissed him. "I didn't. I love you."

His intense gaze held hers. "So why the courage to tell me now?"

She sighed. "So many questions. You should be a cop. Oh wait."

His fingers danced across her ribcage until she squealed with laughter.

Catching her breath she said, "I'm willing to trust God with the details."

"Good because we haven't even begun to talk about the details." He slid the fabric ponytail holders off his fingers, gathered up her fiery hair, and slipped them on. "Promise me something."

"Anything."

"Every morning, for the rest of our lives, you'll put your hair in a ponytail."

Carrie ran her fingers lightly across his temple. "Why?"

"So these little fabric thingies will fall out and I can find them." His smile almost blinded her. He wrapped his hand around her nape and pulled her close. His lips played across her cheek.

Carrie found it hard to think, but she did her best. "Aaron Black...."

"Hmmm?"

She cupped his cheeks and looked into his eyes brimming with love. "Of all the miracles God has sent my way, you are the best miracle of all."

Thank you for reading

Thank you for spending time with Aaron and Carrie. I hope you found encouragement for your own faith journey. If you enjoyed this story be sure and tell your friends. If you have a moment, would you please leave a short review on the site where you purchased *Miracle in Black*? Just a few words will do. Reviews are not only the highest compliment you can pay an author, they also help other readers make informed choices when purchasing books and discovering new authors.

If you haven't yet read my SeaMount Series, continue on to find the first chapter of the first book, OUT OF THE WILDERNESS.

May God bless you and those you love.
Anita

P.S. If you would like to know about new releases and sales, sign up for my newsletter and learn more at my website: anitakgreene.wordpress.com.

Excerpt from

Out of the Wilderness

Book 1 of the SeaMount Series

by

Anita K. Greene

Chapter One

In the murky light of dawn, Grayson Kerr hunkered down in the rough, weedy fringe that separated the logging road from the forest. Suspicion crawled up his back like a hot rash.

Had the SeaMount Agency planted the mini van for him to find? Nothing about the last three days made much sense. A demented Boy Scout obsessed with treasure hunts must have created this wilderness survival trial. The haphazard trek from checkpoint to checkpoint was enough to make a man woods queer.

Gray burrowed a hand beneath the layer of dry grass stuffed between his long sleeve camouflage shirt and tee. The grass made him itch, but at this elevation the added insulation kept him warm. Soft stuffing from the seat of the van would be a welcome improvement, but only if this opportunity to upgrade his stash of survival gear wasn't a lure into a new kind of perdition.

The tang of balsam scented the air. From high in the trees a faint chirp heralded the start of a new day. He unsheathed his knife. The early light softened the angles and edges of the fixed black blade. Hunched low he left the scrub's protection and moved to the front of the van. It had a Rhode Island license plate.

Three nights ago he'd gone to sleep at the SeaMount Agency headquartered in Rhode Island. He awoke the next morning beneath a pine tree in the middle of Nowhere, Maine with a serious case of brain fog. A crude map and instructions were pinned to the tree by the point of his own knife. He'd inspected his watch, knife and every stitch of clothing he wore and still couldn't figure out how SeaMount tracked him. He assumed they had eyes on him to extract him if he ran into trouble. Or worse, became truly lost. That would deep six his chance to work for them. Lost was not an option. He needed the job.

Sidling up on the driver's side, Gray peered into the dim interior. A woman reclined in the driver's seat. She was wrapped in a quilt and sound asleep. Her hair fell in gold ringlets about her attractive face. By the look of her jewelry and manicured fingernails, he'd found himself a real girly girl. What was a woman like her doing out here far from civilization? She should be home cozied up in a warm bed. Was she bait and the girly stuff window dressing? Did SeaMount even *have* female agents?

You're about to find out, Kerr. Gray tightened his grip on the knife keeping it low and out of sight. "Rise and shine, Blondie." He rapped on the window.

She jerked awake. Confusion flickered across her face. Her gaze landed on him. Mouth wide open and tonsils vibrating, she screamed. The confines of the van muted the volume of her voice, but couldn't mask the alarm on her face. Her hand came into view brandishing a heavy flashlight.

Pleased she didn't aim a gun at him, Gray focused on the

back seat where shadowy movement produced thumps and more shrieks of panic.

A small pixie face framed in dark braids pressed against the window.

Gray muttered an expletive. A kid!

Two other faces popped into view. One with ears wired for sound, the other with hair so pale it appeared white in the gloomy interior of the van.

The Agency did things differently for sure, but even they wouldn't involve kids in an exercise like this. Which left only one other option. He'd stumbled on a nest of civilians.

"Go away." The woman shook the flashlight at him.

If he were smart he'd leave. But he'd never figured himself as overly bright. To get what he wanted he'd need to calm them down. Discreetly, he sheathed his knife. "Take it easy. You're safe." The panicked females made the van bounce like a desert patrol vehicle on rough terrain. Gray rubbed a hand across his face. Flakes of swamp mud fell from his three days growth of beard to his dirty shirt lumpy with grass. Not an appearance to inspire trust. He could easily take what he wanted from them. A hard knot formed in his gut. Never before had he preyed on those weaker than him. He didn't like it that the thought enticed him now. More evidence stacked against him for how far he'd slipped towards the darkness lurking inside him.

As a soldier for hire he'd fought stepping across the line separating the good guys from the bad. Six months ago at the hands of an Army medic skilled in treating more than just the body, he'd converted to Christianity. A lot of things can change in six months. To his surprise a man's heart was one of them.

It was that change that brought him here to the north woods pushing through a timed trial, hoping for a job with

SeaMount and the chance to find absolution from the darkness that had become a part of him. Time to leave and reconsider his options while his better self had the upper hand. Frightening women and children wasn't what good guys did.

With a cursory wave he turned back towards the forest.

The metallic roll of the van door opening sliced through the muted wilderness hum.

Knee deep in weeds, Gray whirled around. The pixie ran at him full tilt. Her braids bounced on thin shoulders as her arms pumped hard at her sides.

The driver's door opened. A blood-curdling scream set the hair on his arms upright.

The woman jumped from the vehicle and ran after the little girl. "Andi. Come back here. Andi!" He recognized the terror etched on the woman's face. Too many war zones had burned the gut wrenching fear-filled grimace into his memory.

The pixie took a header and landed at his feet.

Leaning over, Gray helped the youngster up, her arm thin and fragile in his hand. "You okay?"

"Please." Her slight lisp was the result of no front teeth. "You...can't...leave us." Her brown eyes, open and honest, pleaded with him. The anxiety threading through her small voice tightened a burning ball in his gut.

"Oomph." His left side caught the brunt of a body slam. His teeth clacked. Pushing the child away, he went down. Scrub twigs poked his back. Dead leaves crackled beneath his weight. A stone jabbed his hip.

A warm woman sprawled across him.

Not one of those skinny waifs a man might break if he got overenthusiastic with his loving. This one was a real woman. All soft curves and smelling sweet.

Blondie's manicured nails dug into his scalp, cutting the pleasant moment short.

"Hey!" He grabbed her wrist to ease the pain.

Her breath caressed his cheek in hot bursts as she sobbed and fought him. Dodging her other hand, a flurry of movement beyond her shoulder stopped Gray mid motion.

A tiny princess, sparkling tiara askew on her pale hair, peered down at him. He blinked at the vision wondering if he'd hit his head when he fell.

The flat of a hand connected with his cheek in a stinging smack. "Enough!" With a roar, he flipped Blondie to her back. With the bulk of his body he held her to the ground.

The man's hard weight forced the breath from Sophie's lungs as he pressed her into the scratchy weeds. She gasped for air, chest aching, as she twisted and scraped the heel of her sandal the length of his leg. His hot breath seared her neck.

Sophie's vision tunneled to the frightening face staring down at her. *Her girls!* She had to protect them. *God help me.*

Heart ready to burst from her chest and muscles burning, she pummeled him with her fists. Lumps in his shirt made her blows ineffective. She clawed at his hideous face. A chunk fell off in her hand. Revulsion rocketed through her then turned to surprise as the piece crumbled to dust.

He caught her hands in iron fists. She struggled to pull free. Eyes as gray and cold as pond ice raked over her face. His grip tightened.

With a crushing jolt more weight bore down on Sophie as her daughters fell atop the man in a writhing pig pile. His head jerked up in surprise. Arms flailing, legs scrambling, and hair flying like flags of war, they screamed and pulled at his clothing.

He bared his teeth and with a harsh grunt surged up and off of Sophie. She lurched to her feet dragging great gulps of air into her aching lungs.

Her girls held on to him.

Would he take off with her daughters clinging to him? The impending custody battle with their grandparents paled in comparison to losing her girls to this madman.

Sophie grabbed a handful of lavender cloth and yanked. Lissa dropped off landing in the weeds on her backside, one ear bud still intact. The man shook and Hanna fell to the ground, her princess gown tangled about her knees.

Arms wrapped snug around his neck, Andi stuck.

"Andi. Let go!"

Andi tightened her hold. One braid had lost its elastic and come unraveled.

He grasped the arms threatening to cut off his breath.

Sophie's heart lurched. She charged and tore at his hands. "Don't hurt her. Don't you *dare* hurt her!"

He stilled. Behind the mud on his face, his eyes filled with despair. He blinked and the anguish disappeared, replaced by steel.

"Mommy, he's got to stay with us." Andi's chin, smudged with dirt where she'd bumped against the man's filthy neck, rested on a wide muscular shoulder.

"Just let go, honey."

"But we prayed for him last night. Remember?"

His eyes widened with surprise but he said nothing.

"We don't know this man, Andi. He's a stranger. You know the rules about strangers." Every instinct urged Sophie to wrestle her daughter away from him.

"He's our angel, Mommy."

The slack-jawed shock on his face would have been comical had Sophie felt like laughing. A theological discussion with Andi about angels would have to wait.

"Andi. Get. Down. Now."

Indecision flitted across her middle daughter's face. "But we asked God for an angel to keep us safe." Her hands loosened and she slid off. Sneakers hitting the ground she grabbed for his woven fabric belt.

Watchful of the girls, he spoke. "If you're waiting on an angel, you're not waiting on me." His voice, soft and deep, was at odds with his scruffy clothes and the hard eyes that turned to zero in on Sophie. "You're a long way from civilization."

Andi tugged on his belt. "We're lost and our cell phone doesn't work out here."

Sophie's heart hammered in her chest. "Andi, hush."

He swore.

She clamped her lips shut. *Pick your battles, Sophie.* Taking him to task for using bad language in front of the girls could wait.

"Do you have a plan to get out of here?"

Her dignity in the pits, Sophie tried for some semblance of control even if it was only an illusion. She smoothed a hand over her hair and a leaf fell out. She straightened her blouse.

His gaze followed her every move.

"Maybe if I knew where we were." She clasped her hands together to keep them from fluttering like nervous butterflies.

"No." Lissa bolted to her mother's side dragging Hanna with her. Her gaze bounced between the adults.

Eyes on her 'angel' Andi said, "Mommy's not very good with directions."

Sophie's face burned. She wished her daughters weren't so eager to share her shortcomings with a complete stranger.

"Show me your directions."

She crossed her arms taking refuge in belligerence. "I don't have any. I thought I'd remember the way."

"Do you have a GPS?"

She shook her head. Unlike the Acura her late husband Tommy had driven, her van didn't come with a navigation system.

"A map?"

"Yes."

His relieved expression changed to incredulity when Andi piped up. "She can't read it."

Those gray eyes focused on Sophie. "Have you even tried?"

Swiping a hank of hair from her eyes, Sophie ignored the question. They could be sitting smack on top of Mount Katahdin and she wouldn't be able to find their place on the map. "A map won't help. The van is out of gas."

He muttered under his breath and scraped a hand over his face. Dirt sifted to his shirt. "Where are you going?"

She sent another prayer for protection winging heavenward. "Bride Lake."

He glanced at the van before his gaze raked over the girls then shot back to her. "Saw an old sign for the place."

"You did?" Fragments of fear floated away in a wash of relief. "Can we walk there?"

He concealed his surprise behind narrowed eyes. "No way."

"Why not?"

His gaze went straight to Sophie's strappy sandals.

She huffed and jammed her hands on her hips. "We have sneakers."

"What about food and water? I saw the sign three days back."

The fight in Sophie ebbed. "Bottles of water and snacks."

He looked at each girl in turn. "You won't go far on that."

As a child, Sophie had heard the stories about hunters lost in the forest and never found. Years away from the North Woods had dimmed her memory of the unforgiving nature of the wilderness. Getting lost had been her first mistake. Another bad choice could compound her problems and cause the death of someone she loved. She pressed a hand to her stomach. Time to bury her pride. "What do you suggest we do?"

From behind the chunks of dirt on his face, his gaze rested on each of them as though taking their measure. The muscle in his neck pulsed. He shifted his attention to the van.

Time slipped into neutral and idled to the quiet sough of the wind. Even the girls remained motionless as though tagged in a game of Freeze.

The harsh chatter of a whisky jack shattered the quiet.

"I suppose I could guide you."

His enthusiasm was underwhelming. Could she trust him? Did she have a choice?

"If I escort you to the lake you'll do exactly as I say."

Sophie hesitated. Trying to walk out alone could bring disaster. Praying she'd made the right choice she extended her hand, "I'm Sophie Moore."

"Gray Kerr." He enveloped her hand in the warmth and strength of his then turned and surveyed the girls. "You'll follow orders?"

Eyes glued to the play list on her mp3 player, Lissa murmured, "I guess."

Hanna fiddled with her tiara.

He lifted a grungy eyebrow and questioned Andi. "Understood?"

"Yes!" She hopped from one foot to the other eager to get on with the adventure.

Nervous, Sophie pulled Hanna close. "Are you camping?"

"I'm working through a qualifying trial for a job with a security agency."

Not a white-collar job. "What must you qualify in?"

His smile didn't reach his eyes "Survival skills."

Her heart took a nosedive. He didn't have a camp on the other side of the hill or a cooler filled with drinks and breakfast. "And the dirt on your face?"

"Swamp mud. Keeps the black flies at bay."

Still clinging to him, Andi's smile exposed the gummy hole in her mouth. "I told you he's our angel. He knows how to live in the woods." She tugged on his belt. "I'm seven."

His growl didn't dampen her enthusiasm.

Sophie introduced her daughters. "The one hanging on to you is Andi." She pointed to her eldest. "Lissa."

"I'm nine." Lissa tossed Andi a superior glare.

"The little one is Hanna. She's four."

Andi grinned at her angel. "Will we have to eat bugs?"

"Oh, yuck!" Lissa stuck a finger in her mouth and made retching noises.

A brief smile reached his eyes. "Only if you want to."

Also by Anita Greene

OUT OF THE WILDERNESS

INTO THE DEEP

UNDER STARRY SKIES

Learn more about Anita
or sign up for her newsletter at her website:

anitakgreene.wordpress.com

About the Author

Anita became an avid reader the day she discovered the adventures of four little puppies tucked inside a children's book. As a teen, she rewrote the television episodes of her favorite shows. She filled notebooks with what is now called 'fan fiction'. Her stories had more to do with what the heroine wore than with plot.

Many years later Anita decided it was time to put the stories in her head on paper. She attended a workshop advertised by the local library and discovered she enjoyed creating characters and coming up with plots that made their lives difficult. Anita always gives her heroes and heroines a happy ending. They are eternally grateful.